MW01703365

Life and Death in Small-Town America

One Police Officer's Journey

Joseph Patrick Fair

This novel is a work of fiction, loosely inspired in part by some of my experiences as a small-town police officer and firefighter. The names, characters, locations and incidents are fictional, and any resemblance to actual events, places, people or occurrences is coincidental.

ISBN-13: 978-1513627700

ISBN-10: 1513627708

This book would not be possible without my undying faith in God.

I would like to thank my daughter, Jenny and my son, Ryan for their support and encouragement. I would also like to thank my editor, Susan Connelly. It has been a journey.

Chapter 1

Police Officer Joseph Patrick Fair. That's me, and this is my story. The events and cases in this book took place over the course of a decade or so, starting with my entering the police academy. I'm known as 'Joe' to most people, or 'Patty' to my closest friends. I started at the police academy in my mid-thirties and have been a police officer now for about 20 years, handling road patrol and public relations in a small-town police department. I was born into a family of mostly military officers and spent a fair amount of my youth hanging around the VFW Post with my father, grandfather and uncles, listening to stories of their glory days in the military; I suppose that's the genesis of my desire to put on a uniform and help people. My grandfather liked to tell his cronies at the VFW that I was born with the brain of a supercomputer and an imagination that would have put Walt Disney to shame. Clearly, Grandpa was a tad biased and overly proud of his grandson. In reality I'm just a regular, down-to-earth blue-collar guy who lives to serve and protect. I like to think I'm a great cop and hope that others think of me that way. I'm a good father, a pretty good ex-husband, and a loyal friend. My lineage has been traced back to the Scottish Highlands; according to my grandmother, one side of my family has royal Scottish blood. My Grandpa Kennedy once told me that some people have a 'secret sauce' that makes them strive for excellence. He told me that

I'm one of those people. I try to live up to his opinion of me.

I sat in my Chevy truck gazing at the building that would become my second home for the next six months. I was ready; I had no real reason to be hesitating. I just wanted to soak it all in, the whole scene. I wanted to remember everything about the police academy – what it looked like, smelled like, what I felt like as a cadet. I saw other people, presumably my fellow cadets, making their way through the parking lot and into the building, and saw by the clock on my dashboard that I'd better get in there. I didn't want to be the guy who's late the first day.

I opened the door of my truck, almost hitting someone walking past my truck. As I bent down to retrieve the pencil I'd dropped, I said, "I'm sorry; I wasn't watching," just as the other person was saying, "I'm sorry, I wasn't paying attention." We both laughed, and as I stood up I stumbled a little as I stared into the greenest eyes I'd ever seen. I couldn't help it; she was beautiful. No, not just beautiful, I decided. Gorgeous. "Are you…just starting today too?" she asked. "Yes, I'm…I'm Joe. What's your name?" I answered. She stuck out her hand and shook mine, saying, "I'm Gabby. We'd better hurry. Let's go."

Gabriella A. 'Gabby' Bridges. Like me, Gabby was in her mid-thirties when she joined the police academy at the same time I did. She was the only fellow cadet that I completely bonded with and trusted during my training. Gabby was a very beautiful woman, with large green eyes and long, glossy chestnut hair. She had an elegance and an intellectual personality that drew me to her; she was one of the few people who didn't find my passion for studying philosophy odd. The other guys in the academy would rib me about my interest in philosophers, but not Gabby. She was married, but I secretly dreamed about her leaving her husband. Although we took separate career paths after graduating from the academy – Gabby would ultimately end up as lieutenant at the county sheriff's department – we remained good friends throughout our careers.

As Gabby and I walked into the academy and checked in, we were given binders and directed to take a seat in the training room. Gabby walked in ahead of me and took one of two seats together and motioned for me to take the other. I couldn't miss the looks the other guys gave Gabby as she took her seat, and a few knowing glances that were directed my way. As I sat down and got settled in, Sergeant Larry Wallace entered the room and introduced himself. He had a presence that was larger than life, and what he had to tell us would stick with me forever.

"Police work creates a brotherhood like no other," said Sergeant Wallace. "When you bond with people under extreme pressure, the emotional energy is different than that of family, marriage or business. The immediacy of life and death causes people to form thought patterns that do not come naturally. The difference between life and death can be fractions of a second, relying on each other for survival. The relationships between officers become quintessential partnerships."

He continued, "The administrators at the police academy are looking for character, strength and determination, as well as steady predictability under extreme stress. Just showing up to the police academy can be overwhelmingly intimidating, even terrifying for some people."

> *Deputy Sheriff Sergeant Larry Wallace. In his early fifties, the sergeant was like a character out of a 1960s-era police TV show. Larry was 6'3" and 225 pounds of muscle with light brown hair and blue eyes. An intimidating and commanding presence in any room, his energy was palpable. He was the perfect person to oversee continuing education and advanced training.*

I was at first taken aback by Larry's imposing presence, but I soon came to respect him completely. Larry didn't go around fucking with people, but you knew better than to give him a hard time. Some people exude so much attitude that they rarely have to speak. Larry's silent message was "don't fuck with me."

Larry had started his career working as a sheriff down in Texas 25 years previously. On his 14th day on the job, he was involved in a high-speed chase and a gunfight, took three shots to his vest and had to kill the assailant. There was no doubt – Larry was the real deal.

Larry told us, "You cadets need something that we, the police academy, have. We're going to make you pay for it with sweat and pain. You'll have to earn that badge and gun. You must show us you have all the right stuff, or we'll kick you out and it will be billboarded among your peers that you are a loser. We're going to run you up and down hills; we're going to scare you like you've never been scared before; we're going to put you through the most painful and stressful few months of your life. If you pass all the tests you just might be a cop someday."

My first day at the police academy, I got acquainted with the other cadets. None of them had previously completed the fire academy, as I had. It gave me the advantage of some experience and training that would transfer over. I had completed first aid and CPR training and was working as a volunteer for my local fire department.

Of all the friends I made as a cadet, Gabby became my best friend throughout our time in the academy. We often studied together, and we quickly found that we were well-matched in intelligence, drive, purpose and motivation. The other guys in the academy assumed that I became close friends with Gabby only because she was so beautiful, but it was her personality and intelligence that really interested me. I wasn't blind; I could see that she was gorgeous, but my main interest was in finding a study partner, a confidante and a lifeline.

At the academy, there are challenges in physical fitness, scholastic ability, marksmanship, precision driving, tactical response, and prisoner detention; above all, there is the challenge of earning the respect of your instructors.

Sergeant Larry appeared to really like teaching the proper use of the Taser and pepper spray. Later I learned why; this is the most painful aspect of training, and it satisfied Larry's sadistic need to inflict a little pain every now and then. I couldn't help but think of him as "Sergeant Pepper" while we were doing the pepper spray drills, and I couldn't get that song out of my head. I kept that to myself, though; all I needed was for him to hear that I'd called him Sergeant Pepper. I'd be out on my ass. Thirty percent of the students wash out during Taser and pepper spray training. For those who don't wash out, once your instructors and peers see that you're able to manage the intense pain of those drills, they gain a measure of respect for you. The drills brought about a bonding between the instructors and students that felt almost magical. After experiencing the pain involved in the pepper spray and Taser exercise, I felt confident that I could use them on the street to defend public safety.

Cops get involved in police work for any number of reasons. Personally, I wanted to make a change in my community. I saw things that disturbed me and thought that I could fix them. To what degree I could make an impact was unclear.

Chapter 2

After putting in every ounce of energy and determination that I possessed, I graduated from the police academy at the top of my class. I was hired into a small village department and was introduced to the chief, the lieutenant and the training officer.

> *Chief Dennis David Michaels. In his late sixties, the Chief of Police had a classic, distinguished appearance and a chiseled face; he looked every bit the part of a police chief. Clearly the blood coursing through his veins ran red, white and blue. He appeared to possibly be of Scandinavian descent, with light hair, fair skin and blue eyes. Average in height and weight, his uniform fit him like it had been custom-tailored – and it probably had been.*

I didn't ask the chief about it, but by looking at the plaques on the wall of his office, it was clear that he had been discharged from the Army with honors and that he had spent some time in Vietnam. More than likely those experiences had shaped part of his life. Some members of the department talked about him as though he were a ticking time bomb, but I wouldn't see that side of him for a while.

After about 15 minutes' discussion with the chief, I realized that I was working for the right supervisor, which doesn't always happen. It just felt like the right fit – me, the chief, this particular village police department, everything. The chief said I would need equipment and guidance, and he turned me over to Lieutenant Davison.

> *Lieutenant Isaac Daniel Davison, better known as 'Lieutenant Dan'. In his late thirties, Lieutenant Dan had spent his entire adult life working for the U.S. Marine Corps Reserve and as a full-time police officer. He fit the stereotypical image of a Marine. He had spiky blonde hair and blue eyes. At 5'10" and 170 pounds of lean and curved muscles, no one in the department fit the image better. Lieutenant Dan had a proclivity for discussions of little intellectual depth, which sometimes led people to think he was stupid. That was not the case; he was very book smart but just didn't have the gift of carrying on conversations of substance.*

If you've ever seen the Marine Corps recruitment TV commercial, you may have noticed the guy coming out of the back of the helicopter with an M5 machine gun in his hand. This guy could be the lieutenant; the resemblance is remarkable. A few times I've seen the commercial and thought, "What the fuck…that's my Lieutenant Dan!"

Lieutenant Dan issued equipment, instructions, and rules to be followed or else. He reminded me that I was on probation and could be released without explanation at any time. After he had me fill out a lot of paperwork, he introduced me to my field training officer.

Steven Matthew Weinberg, Field Training Officer. Everyone called him 'Maverick'. In his mid-thirties, Steve Weinberg was a second-generation police officer whose mother had broken boundaries and earned her way into the police department in the early 1980s. Maverick described himself as half Dutch and half British. I figured that meant he was a little cheap, and snobby about it. He was a fine gentleman, a man of impeccable character and integrity. He stood six feet tall with piercing blue eyes, brown hair and a rather large square jaw reminiscent of Dudley Do-Right from the Rocky and Bullwinkle cartoon. Maverick had a need to strive for perfection; as a result, he was always obsessing about improvements and corrections.

"How'd you get the nickname 'Maverick', anyway?" I asked one day. He said, "Watch out, stand by, get out of my way, and be advised – I'm in charge." His intellectual capacity was near-genius and when he spoke, he was articulate and precise. When he walked into a room he knew he was the smartest guy and often needed to show that to other people.

I took to my field training officer like a brother, and we bonded in the cruiser. He often remarked that I knew his next action and prepared for it before he would make a move. He was very quick-witted, and we had a near-constant banter going on. We both enjoyed this verbal dueling. On occasion we would get into a philosophical debate and lose our focus on traffic enforcement. At these times we would need to go have lunch and refocus.

It's difficult to explain to what degree police officers are competitive. There isn't a simple answer. They always have each other's backs, but at the same time, they also have their own images to manage and polish. If your actions or words tarnish another police officer's reputation, he or she will let you know with a kind statement along the lines of, "You either shut the fuck up or else." Reputation is everything in this game; making rank, making money, and making a legacy are very important to most police officers.

In a small police department, the chief and the lieutenant are constantly trying to manage the department's image. When a good cop puts on a positive face for the police department, this increases the likelihood that funding, equipment and respect will flow into the police department like a river of gold. A bad cop, on the other hand, can be counted upon to damage the image of the department, whether permanently or temporarily.

Such a situation puts both the chief and lieutenant in the hot seat, threatening them with possible removal from their highly-prized positions. This creates tremendous stress and pressure on a police department that is trying to determine whether a rookie is ready to hit the streets. It is clearly a very critical decision that must be weighed carefully.

When the rookie is deemed street-ready, the chief typically sits down with the rookie and says something like, "I want you to hit the streets for the next 90 days, do the job to the best of your ability, and most of all, generate no complaints from citizens. If you do, I will need to investigate you and possibly terminate your employment." Then he will get the rookie pumped up and as confident as possible, saying that he believes you're ready, the ball is in your court, and you make your own destiny.

When the chief, Lieutenant Dan and Maverick all decided that I was ready to hit the streets solo, it was one of my proudest career moments. I finally felt like a real cop, like I had earned the trust of my superiors and had been accepted into their ranks. I belonged. The day they told me that I was street-ready and would be on my own the next day, I managed to stay cool until I got into the privacy of my truck. There I pumped my fist and shouted, "Yes! Yes, yes, yes!" without anyone there to witness my embarrassing display of emotion. On the way home that day, I stopped at the store and picked up the best New York strip steak they had, and some sides to go with it. I was going to go home, put on some music and grill up a little celebration.

Chapter 3

After setting up my equipment in my cruiser, checking and rechecking all policies, filling my briefcase with forms and procedures, and studying all possible contingency plans, I was finally ready to hit the streets.

I did what most cops do on their first day on the streets – I bought lunch for my field training officer, Maverick, and asked him all about his own first day. We sat in the restaurant and he explained to me that if you aren't scared, you're not in touch with reality. Maverick advised me to go out in the community and ask the people how I could help make the village a better place for all its citizens. I took his advice; I went around solo to many of the local businesses, introduced myself and handed out my business cards, letting them know that I was there to serve their needs.

One business that I called on that first day was Daily's DrugMart, one of the town's two pharmacies. The owner and head pharmacist, Bob Daily, was happy to meet me. He came down from his elevated perch in the pharmacy and offered me a cold soda from his old-fashioned soda fountain. He told me it was one of only a handful remaining anywhere; he'd found it in an old pharmacy up north that had gone out of business, bought it, fixed it up and installed it in his store. It was quaint and drew in some pharmacy business for him, because customers could sit and enjoy a cup of coffee or a cold drink while they waited for their prescriptions to be filled.

Bob got us a couple of cold drinks, and we sat at the deserted counter of the soda fountain. We chatted about how business was going, about how I liked the town, about pretty much everything but whatever it was it seemed he had on his mind. I just had a feeling he wanted my help with something. Finally, he moved in a little closer and said in a quiet voice, "Officer Fair, we might have a problem on our hands here." "Oh?" I responded. "What's going on?" Bob told me that he and the owner of the other pharmacy in town had a very good business relationship, helping each other out when needed, and letting each other know when they thought there was some sort of a prescription drug scam going on. Occasionally a shady customer who had never been in before would present a suspicious-looking prescription to be filled, and if Bob turned the customer away, he'd call the other pharmacy in town to warn them. Inevitably the scammer would try both stores and would leave empty-handed because one pharmacist would call and warn the other to be on the lookout. "Sounds like a pretty good system you've got going there," I said. Bob agreed, saying, "We may be competitors, but we're professionals and friends; neither of us wants to see the other get scammed." "How can I help?" I asked.

Bob told me that many of the prescriptions he refused to fill were for large quantities of opioids; furthermore, the prescriptions were being written by one doctor in particular. "I don't know exactly what his scam is – selling prescriptions to addicts or maybe dealers, maybe some insurance fraud too – but these are not my normal customers. They're not local, no one knows them, and they look shifty. Just a few months ago, a little boy found a handgun on one of my shelves and asked his mother to buy it for him. She saw that it was not a toy – it was a real gun – and she brought it to me. I called your colleague, Officer Weinberg, and he came right down to pick it up and ask the little boy and his mother some questions. Apparently, it was unregistered, and the serial number had been filed off. Worse yet, it was loaded. That little boy could have been killed, or killed someone else, playing with what he thought was a toy gun. I'm certain it was somehow lost or left behind by one of these scammers. I don't just want them out of my drugstore, I want them out of this town. Anything you can do to help make that happen?" I told him I'd have to investigate the situation further and promised to talk to Officer Weinberg – Maverick – when I got back to the station, so he could brief me on the case. "I'll be back in touch with you, Bob. If there's some kind of illegal opioid scheme going on, I don't want that in this town either. I'll be back in touch." We shook hands as I thanked him for the cold soda, and he said, "There's always a cold drink or a hot cup of coffee for you officers. I like having you guys stop in; makes my legitimate customers feel safe and maybe keeps a bad guy away every now and then. I'll look forward to seeing you soon."

When I got back to the station at the end of the day, I told Maverick about my visit with Bob Daily at the pharmacy and asked about the gun the little boy had found. Maverick told me pretty much everything Bob had said, but the information about the doctor was news to him. He was very interested to hear that all the sketchy prescriptions were being written by one doctor, and for unusually large quantities of opioids. "You know," said Maverick, "we've had an uptick in opioid overdoses over the past several months, and it's not just the typical drug addicts. We've had several high school students –

otherwise good kids – OD on prescription drugs. This is becoming a real problem, and I'd like to find out how they're getting their hands on these drugs. You and I can work on it together, but it's my case. You're just getting your feet wet."

Chapter 4

I had started to get to know a few of the old-timers. These guys were a treasure trove of wisdom and kept me from going off the rails. The old guys always seemed to say the same things – back in the day, things were much simpler; we would fix things completely, even if it was frequently painful and ugly; today we put Band-Aids over problems and hope they will go away – but even though the advice was old, it was new to me. I soaked it all in, every word of it, because I knew that these guys knew their stuff and had my best interests at heart.

> *Nate B. Smith, otherwise known as 'The Joker'. In his early seventies, Nate was a part-timer who worked special events. Nate was a tall, thin, old Dutch guy with very thin, snow-white hair that just barely covered the tops of his ears. His face showed every one of his 70 years, with large white teeth that appeared to be about one and a half times the size they should be. Nate had spent most of his life working in management for a large pharmaceutical company. He worked weekends for the police department, more as a hobby than as a job. Known for the most disgusting dirty jokes, he truly was more a joker than a cop. Nate suggested that if I ever had a bad day, I should just swing by his house and talk; he lived only a couple of blocks from the police station. Many of the officers were in the habit of stopping by Nate's house to hang out in*

his tricked-out garage, which housed a world-class '57 Chevy street rod with a monster V8 engine. His garage was the epitome of a 'man cave', with a refrigerator full of beverages and a constant supply of home-baked treats made by his wife.

Nate liked to tell a story about when he was a rookie officer. He'd found an old wooden box on the side of the road and brought it into the briefing room. Just as the sergeant was about to open the box, he spotted some wires protruding from one side. He immediately called the bomb squad, which found a booby trap made up of four sticks of dynamite. After that, Nate liked to say that you could never be too safe.

Marty A. Norris. Marty liked to say the A stood for "Angler". Like Nate, Marty was also in his early seventies and was a part-timer. He had a sort of John Wayne-like, cowboy look going on, with attitude and swagger to spare. Marty had worked for a large public safety department. After he retired, he got bored and came to work in the village. Marty had two favorite topics of conversation – Canadian fishing trips and bedding beautiful women. The fish stories were true but, unfortunately for Marty, the women were nothing more than wishful thinking. Marty's advice was simple – when in doubt, ask your supervisor; always call for backup, no exceptions; and if you screw up, tell your supervisor immediately so he or she can provide damage control.

I decided one day to stop by Nate's garage. He'd told me to stop by any time I wanted to talk, whether I needed advice or just wanted to shoot the shit, but until now I'd been a little too intimidated to just show up like everyone else seemed to do. "C'mon, Patty," I thought to myself. "Grow up, grow a pair and start acting like you belong." After my shift was over, since I didn't have the kids that day and had nothing pressing to do at home, I decided to stop in. I was in luck; both Nate and Marty were hanging out in Nate's garage, drinking a cold beer and talking about how things were different back in the day.

"Joe! It's about time you came by," Nate called out. "Get in here and grab a cold one and tell us what's been going on. You off duty?" When I said that I was, Nate said, "Good. Over here's the fridge, and you can help yourself to anything, any time. No beer when you're on duty, of course, but I think you'll find something you like in there whether you're on the clock or not." With that, Nate opened the refrigerator door, revealing a very impressive array of a few different beers, various soft drinks and bottled water. Nate and Marty both came around to shake my hand and make me feel welcome, and my nerves began to calm down. I told them about some of the recent happenings around the station and about my going around town introducing myself to business owners like Bob Daily and others.

Nate offered me some of his wife's legendary cookies, saying, "Nancy, my wife, isn't home right now or I'd introduce you. She always likes to meet the new officers. She keeps us stocked up out here with cookies and snacks, probably to keep us in the garage and out of her hair. These chocolate chip cookies here are her specialty. She uses three different kinds of chocolate in them – milk chocolate, semisweet chocolate and dark chocolate – and I keep telling her she needs to go into business selling them." I took a bite of one and was in heaven; I told Nate, "Please tell Nancy for me that these are the best chocolate chip cookies I've ever tasted. I'm looking forward to meeting her. If she ever needs a guinea pig for new recipes, you know where to find me." Nate said, "Now if we could just find a woman like Nancy for Marty. You know, a real woman, not one of those imaginary women he's always talking about. Are you married, Joe?" I replied that I had been married but was now divorced, but that our twins had made it all worth it. I pulled out my wallet to show the guys photos of my kids, and we talked about our families for a while.

Marty asked me how I felt things were going at the station – whether I felt like I was fitting in, whether I felt well-prepared to hit the streets – and I told him and Nate that I thought things were going as well as they possibly could. I said that Maverick, the chief and Lieutenant Dan all seemed happy with my performance, and Marty said, "Just remember that different cops have different personalities, so you need to consider their age, experience, rank and their perspective of what needs to be corrected in society. All of these inform an officer's judgment, behavior and ideas." I nodded in agreement, and Nate added, "What makes the chief happy may not be what makes Maverick happy, and what Maverick's looking for may not be what Lieutenant Dan is looking for. You're serving three masters, and you have to learn to juggle all three of them and their needs."

"But don't let us get you all nervous," said Marty. "If everyone seems happy with you – and I haven't heard anything to the contrary – then you're probably managing to juggle them already." I took a small sip of the beer Nate had handed me when I got there – I wasn't much of a drinker, but every now and then I'd have a drink to be sociable – and asked, "You guys would let me know if you ever heard I'd dropped one of the balls I'm juggling, wouldn't you?" They both said that they would, if they weren't breaking a confidence by telling me. Marty said, "Cops usually keep their cards pretty close, as you've probably noticed by now, and if one tells you something in confidence, you just don't ever want to break that confidence because if cops can't trust each other with information, how can they trust each other with their lives?"

Nate and Marty had given me a lot to think about already, so I changed the subject. "Hey, Nate, tell me about this beauty of a car here." And with that, Nate was off and running. He could talk about that car for hours – all the restoration he'd done, how long it took, how much each part cost him – and the rest of the time I was there it was all about the car. Well, the car and a little bit of Marty's big fish stories. It wasn't possible to have a conversation with Marty without hearing about fish.

"Did I ever tell you about that whopper of a steelhead I caught up in British Columbia a few years back? Had to have been 20 pounds, at least. I fought with that fish for close to an hour before I finally reeled it in." Marty had a faraway look as he recounted the story. "And after fishing, my buddy and I got cleaned up and went into town for some dinner and the women in that town…I'm tellin' ya, I – "Marty was cut off by Nate, who was saying, "Yeah, yeah, yeah…heard this one several times. Every time, the fish gets bigger and the women get hotter. Joe, you ever heard any of Marty's stories?" "I've heard a few," I said. "So just how hot were these women?" Nate threw his head back and laughed, and said, "Please, don't get him started. He'll go on all night."

"On that note," I said, "I should get home, get some dinner and hit the sack. I've got an early day tomorrow. Thanks for the beer and the laughs!" As I headed to my truck, Nate called after me, "Hey, Joe, come by any time." "Will do," I called back to him. I drove home feeling like I'd just taken a big step toward becoming one of the guys instead of the new guy. It was a good feeling.

Chapter 5

At lunch with Maverick one day, he was in full-on Field Training Officer mode. He was lecturing me, "When you're dispatched to a call, you must consider that there is a prosecuting attorney somewhere in the office who really doesn't know what's going on. You're communicating a life event. You've gotta put it down on paper to the best of your ability and then explain to the prosecuting attorney who the good guy, the bad guy and the victim are. You know?" I was eating my burger, nodding my understanding.

Maverick went on, "It isn't as easy as it looks in a Hollywood movie, with multiple camera angles and skillful editing and production. In real life, a cop has to get a narrative down on paper. The narrative must be as multidimensional as possible and capture the depth and gravity of the situation, so the prosecutor has everything he or she needs to go to court and effectively make a case. Know what I mean?" I nodded again, my mouth too full to answer.

He picked up his burger and I thought he was done with the lecture, but he put it back down and continued, "A really good cop is like a beat reporter with a photographic memory and a meticulous, laser-focused eye for detail. Not all cops have these gifts; as a result, some cases end up plea-bargained, with the defendant getting only a fraction of the jail time that he or she deserves." Finally, Maverick took a bite of his burger and said, "I'd better get to eating this burger before it's cold." I appreciated the information, but I wasn't in the mood for a dissertation at the moment. I'd been brooding all morning because when I picked the kids up from their mother's the night before, they were full of questions about whether I was going to give little old ladies tickets like Mommy had said. I was trying to figure out how to address it with my ex and how to handle it with my two innocent little kids. I wanted to preserve their innocence as long as possible, and they didn't need to be worrying about Daddy going around being mean to elderly ladies.

Maverick said, "Patty, pay attention. This field training is important, and I need you to be all in. Police work is serious business; your frame of mind can mean the difference between life and death." "I'm sorry I zoned out on you for a minute," I replied. "I won't let it happen again." He asked what was on my mind, and I gave him the short version of what had happened with the twins. "You've got to compartmentalize, Patty," said Maverick. If you're out there on the street distracted by your personal life, you could get killed. You gotta be all in when you're on the job. It's not easy, but you just have to learn to wall off your personal issues when you're on duty." I apologized again, saying that I really had heard everything Maverick had been lecturing about and that I'd work on keeping my private life out of my head while on duty.

Then Maverick gave me some news that perked me up considerably. Apparently, the chief had a case he wanted to assign to me, and he'd asked Maverick to make sure I was ready to work a case on my own – hence the intensified field training lecture today. Maverick wanted to make sure I wouldn't embarrass him and make him look like he hadn't prepared me properly to work a case. I was excited to get started and asked Maverick, "So tell me! What kind of a case is it?", but Maverick just said,

"You'll have to go back to the station and talk to the chief. He'll assign it to you, give you what information he has on it so far, and he'll want to talk to you to make sure you know how to work up this case properly. Just make sure you have your head in the game, okay? I don't want you making me look bad." I promised him that I was, as he put it earlier, 'all in'.

We finished our lunch, and I insisted on paying for Maverick's because I felt guilty about disrespecting him by not giving him my undivided attention when he was trying to prepare me for my first case. Maverick snickered a little and said, "If it gets you to buy me lunch, maybe I should let you ignore me more often." With that, we headed back to the station so I could meet with the chief to get my first case assigned to me. I couldn't help feeling like I was finally a real cop, with a real case to work. It felt good.

Chapter 6

I had hoped that my first case would be an exciting, high-profile case, but to my great disappointment, that was not what the chief assigned to me. My first case was a malicious destruction of property involving two automobiles in one driveway. After talking with the chief to get what details he had and to make sure he felt I was ready to work my own case, I was dispatched to 409 Clinton Avenue.

I knocked on the door and it was answered by a 48-year old man who said that he'd had conflicts with a former resident of his home. He believed that the previous night, the former resident had smashed the windows out of his cars and punctured the tires. He went on to state that he had full coverage insurance on both vehicles and provided me with the appropriate documentation – identification, registration, proof of insurance and license plates. "Can you catch the SOB that wrecked my cars?", he asked. "He would have to pay my insurance company restitution, and that would make me real happy."

I asked him if he had security cameras or knew of anybody who had witnessed the malicious destruction of his vehicles, but he said no. He did say that the lady down at the end of the street was "a real nosy bitch". After taking pictures and writing a report, I started an official investigation and issued a complaint number. I talked to a few of his neighbors, who all backed up his claim that the previous resident of the house was known to be violent and mentally unstable.

I didn't want to bother the neighbor at the end of the street; but later that day, as I was driving by doing traffic enforcement, she waved me down to tell me that there was trouble in the neighborhood and that she knew all the details.

She said that the previous night, around 11:00, she had been walking her dog in front of her house. She said that she had seen a large blue Ford F-150 truck traveling southbound on Clinton Avenue, and believed that it was driven by Mr. Jones, the former resident of the house where the cars had been vandalized. When I asked her if she'd had any previous interactions with Mr. Jones, she stated that she had not, but that she had no respect for him and that he was known to be disagreeable most of the time. I looked up Mr. Jones on the Department of Motor Vehicles database. He owned a Ford F-150 truck, with up-to-date registration, title and plates, and with a new address added to his registration. I decided to pay him a visit.

After introducing myself to Mr. Jones, I told him that he was a person of interest in a malicious destruction of property investigation and that he did not have to answer my questions. I advised him of his Miranda rights and asked him if he wanted to give me a statement. He stated he had nothing to hide because he didn't "fuck up" the vehicles at his previous residence. He said that his former roommate was out to get him and had evicted him without cause. Near the end of the conversation, I asked him if he had ever had any encounters with a woman who lived at the end of the block on Clinton Street. "Yeah," he said, "I was married to that bitch 25 years ago."

This case had many conflicts of interest. I wanted to prove myself and find the person who was responsible for this crime; this is when I met Bill Eastwood.

> *Detective William Samuel 'Bill' Eastwood. In his early forties, Detective Bill Eastwood was a traffic cop/detective. A rather short and stout man, about 5'7" and 200 pounds, Bill had big shoulders and a thick, muscular torso. He was swarthy, possibly of Italian or Greek heritage, with his dark brown hair and olive-colored eyes. He was known to be a man of few words, but when he did speak it was all business. Bill was one of the other guys on the department who was cross-trained for firefighting and EMS; he was highly accomplished and well-respected within the department.*

Bill acted as both road patrolman and detective depending on what the department needed. His heart was in detective work, but in a small town, there weren't always a lot of cases to work.

Bill advised me, "When you work a case in a small town, generally everybody knows everybody else's business. The best you can do is try to separate the facts from the bullshit, get it down on paper and get it in front of the prosecutor. He or she might know even more than you, so just don't overthink it; get it down, get it to the prosecutor, and move on to your next case." I followed Bill's instructions and later received an email saying the prosecutor's office was reviewing the case. Late that night I woke up and started thinking, "Section 750.377a,

Act 328 of 1931 – did I fill out that charging request properly?"

I sought out Bill the next day to talk about my case. I wanted to make sure I was doing everything he would do. "Hey, Bill…have you got a minute? I'd like to pick your brain." Bill said, "Sure, but just give me five minutes to finish up this report. I'll come and find you when I'm done." I nodded my thanks and went back to my desk to look over the case file and make sure I knew all the details by heart. In a few minutes, Bill came by and went over the file with me – the facts, what I had done, what questions I had asked and of whom – and he told me that I'd done a great job working the case. The chief walked by and asked what we were working on, and Bill said, "Joe just wanted me to look over his case and see if there was anything he'd missed, but his work looks really complete to me." The chief nodded in satisfaction and kept walking, and I was flooded with relief that a detective like Bill thought I'd done a good job on my first case and that the chief knew about it.

Chapter 7

Maverick had told me that the reality of police work is that instinct and good judgment are necessary in order to have a successful day, and that a rookie officer struggles to find this balance. I found this to be true. One day while on patrol I noticed a car parked in the 'no parking' zone in front of the local pizza joint. I decided to go into the pizza place and ask the owner of the car to move it into a marked parking spot. When I found the woman who had parked her car there, she said, in a snippy tone, "Don't you have anything more important to do than bother me?" "I have many things to do today, Ma'am" I replied, "but I'm not moving on to them until you move your vehicle, or I will have to write you a ticket." She snapped, "You must be new to the department; once I talk to the chief he's going to have your ass." I said, "How about if I write a ticket to you and a ticket to the chief for obstruction of justice, then?" She just shook her head and said, in a haughty voice, "Please excuse me; I need to move my car."

A few minutes after I left the pizza joint, I was dispatched to a three-car accident near Washington on Vine Street. I heard via the radio that Maverick was clearing his current call. Three minutes later he arrived on the scene. I gave him a quick briefing and he took over the scene.

I was given the assignment of getting information from the driver of a blue Pontiac. After getting the driver's paperwork I passed it on to Maverick. Moments later, the fire department arrived on the scene. I spoke with Deputy Fire Chief Mack Dudley.

Mack W. 'Big Mack' Dudley. In his early fifties, he had been Deputy Fire Chief for ten years. Most of the department members believed that Mack had 'issues'. At times, he'd been called a sick, twisted egomaniac. At fire calls he could be unpredictable. His professionalism diminished during times of extreme stress. How he made the rank of deputy fire chief was unknown; some thought he must have dirt on the fire chief.

Out of the passenger side of the fire truck hopped Little Mack.

Mack W. 'Little Mack' Dudley Jr. In his mid-twenties, Little Mack looked just like his father but was totally opposite in personality. Little Mack avoided arguments and was shy. He gave orders at fire scenes like he was unsure of himself, which left his fellow firefighters reluctant to follow his directions. This, of course, enraged Big Mack. If offended, at some point in the rescue Big Mack would have a meltdown and Little Mack would cringe.

Out of the back seat jumped the infamous Glen Rawlings.

Glen T. 'Throw 'em in the River' Rawlings. A firefighter in his late thirties, Glen was one of the most fun and colorful characters on the fire department – never a dull moment, never afraid of a dare, always pranking. He was always ready to throw someone in the river if they pissed him off. Glen looked like a professional football player but acted more like a professional wrestler.

At this scene we had three vehicles and four people injured, with one requiring extrication from the vehicle. As more members of the fire department arrived on the scene, it resembled an action-packed adventure drama, with firefighters and police officers working in concert to effect a successful rescue. At times I felt overwhelmed by the sheer magnitude of the physical injuries.

I saw Maverick on the radio calling for more resources and personnel, a call for mutual aid from surrounding communities.

During the operation a few mistakes were made that caused the progress of the rescue to take longer than expected. Near the end of the rescue, Maverick called a huddle and all personnel agreed to meet afterward at the firehouse. After we got back to the police station and completed our reports, Maverick said, "Let's head down to the firehouse for a post-incident review of the scene." When we got there, Big Mack was in the training room drawing a diagram of the intersection.

After a few exchanges between Maverick and the Big Mack, there were differing opinions about the proper positions in which to park the police cars and the fire truck. Maverick kept saying, "This position is the safest." Mack kept saying, "My position is the most effective position for vehicles considering the ambulances haven't arrived." Things were getting heated in the training room. I knew that neither of them was good at admitting mistakes.

I suggested a compromise. "How about we set up a mock training next week and try both methods?" Mack looked at me contemptuously and shook his head. Then Maverick said, "Fuck that shit." Finally, both agreed to disagree and walked out of the training room.

Chapter 8

Of all the things I was taught at the police academy, the force continuum, and limitations on the use of force, were what they spent the most time on. This is where I met the sheriff.

> *County Sheriff Richard E. Anderson, Jr. Rick was one of the most respected individuals in law enforcement in the county. He was elected by one of the highest margins of any sheriff, and everybody loved the guy. He had an unusual comfort zone around him. I always thought Rick looked like Chuck Norris without a beard.*

The sheriff showed up the day of the test and said, "If you can't get this, I will never deputize you." Explaining the force continuum requires a very large diagram showing the various levels of threat perception, starting with strategic threat at the bottom of the diagram and moving upward through tactical, volatile, harmful and lethal threats.

The sheriff explained, "The challenge lies in knowing when the situation calls for changing gears. There is a gray area called situational awareness. Some officers feel more fear, which ratchets up the gear changes, while a calmer officer might get caught on the drop because he's too trusting. The right training and experience can fix this problem."

Shortly after my training, I experienced a call that showed me the importance of the force continuum.

Making a traffic stop late one night, I approached a vehicle in which there were two rather small, young teen girls. I expected them to be afraid of me. To my surprise, the driver jumped out and stuck her lit cigarette into my face just below my left eye. The other girl ran around the cruiser and started kicking me in the shins. I was startled, but neither girl was trying to pull my gun from my duty belt.

They were trying to get me to let them go. I grabbed the arm of the closer girl and twisted it behind her back, quickly putting both of her arms together and speed-cuffing her. I pushed the second girl back on the ground, rolled her over and hit her with the second cuffs. As I jumped back up off the ground, checking the scene for more unfriendlies, I noticed that the first girl was frozen in pain. Clearing my eyes, I saw that her forearm was fractured. The outer radial bone by the right wrist had a greenstick fracture, where the bone was sticking out of the skin. Her arm looked really bad. I tried to figure out how she could have sustained the fracture but wasn't sure. It was possible she'd struck the cruiser on the way down to the ground; surely there was no way that my grabbing her arm and putting it behind her back could have caused this injury. The second girl yelled, "You almost killed my friend Sarah, you shitty cop!" I said calmly, "If you attack a police officer, you need to expect a fight." Crying now, she replied, "Well, Sarah has a felony warrant and when we got out of the car she said to do whatever it takes to get away." I asked where her parents were, and she looked down, mumbling that they were dead and that she didn't want to talk about it. "What about Sarah's parents?", I asked, and she said, "I think they're dead too." I immediately called Lieutenant Dan and said, "I could use some help here."

Before I knew it, Lieutenant Dan was there saying, "Let's get these girls in my cruiser so I can hear their story." After listening to them, he said, "There are a lot of holes in this story. Let's look at the dash cam from your cruiser." We both got into my cruiser and I rewound the tape. The tape showed that Sarah had tried to pull my gun from my duty belt; this would change the proper amount of force to be used in an arrest. I noticed that in my adrenaline rush, I had squeezed her wrist strongly, which may have caused the injury. The lieutenant said, "Off the record, it was two against one and if she'd gone for my gun, I would have gone straight to lead on her. Your use of force was totally appropriate, and I'll let the chief know that you did all the right things for all the right reasons." He added, "Dub a copy of the tape in case this goes to court, and call a second ambulance because the burn under your eye is starting to bleed. Now I have fill out an accident report."

I immediately got on the radio. The fire department and EMS showed up and gave me a hard time for letting a little 5'1", 90-pound girl beat me up.

I contacted Sarah's aunt and explained that she was on her way to the hospital with an injury. "How did she break her arm?", asked the aunt. I said that she had broken her arm when she was being arrested. "Arrested for what?", the aunt demanded. I said that Sarah had a felony warrant and was going to be charged with assault on a police officer.

Chapter 9

After a few years of police work you think you've seen everything, but in reality, you're just starting to learn. You are at the bottom of the learning curve. Most criminals are pretty stupid and catching them is a matter of out-thinking them; but occasionally you'll come across a criminal who is a genius. The match of wits is the challenge I live for, the ultimate chess game that can possibly end in life or death.

During a briefing from the area's state police, they explained to me that a big-time drug dealer was coming in and out of my jurisdiction. They had him under surveillance and I was not to interfere with their investigation or blow their undercover officer's cover. When I asked for the undercover officer's name and description they told me, "That's on a 'need to know' basis and you do not need to know."

About two weeks later, on a traffic stop, I got a tip that there was a person dealing drugs from one of the abandoned buildings downtown. I briefly thought about calling the state police but figured there was no way it could be the same person. During a preliminary tour of the building, I encountered a homeless man. He did not look at me with fear; it was different. He looked up, then down, then from side to side and behind him. I asked him his name and he replied, in a very low voice, "FOP." I said, testing him, "Oh – S.P. Narc Post 53." "No," he said, "Post 51." Clearly, he was the undercover officer the state police had been so unwilling to identify.

State Police Trooper "You can call me 'Tommy'". Narcotics undercover officer.

I said, "Thanks. Glad you corrected me. I got briefed by your CO at the 51. I'll back out; happy hunting." Many times, communication can make or break a case. Good communication is simple, timely and precise. In this case, the last thing 'Tommy' needed was another cop hanging around making conversation with him when he was undercover.

About a week later, Tommy, the undercover state police narcotics cop, walked into my police station. We had a long and detailed conversation during which he explained to me that the drug dealer coming in and out of the police district was very sophisticated. The abandoned building was booby-trapped. He was looking for some help from the community. I got on the phone and called a few people to ask if they might be interested in some unofficial brainstorming. We met one night at the local diner to have dinner and discuss all the aspects of the case. Once we had come to a full understanding of the case we realized that we had our hands full. The standard sting operation was not going to work on this guy. We realized that he had the building booby-trapped with safe rooms, explosives and military-style weapons. Trying to raid the building and capture him, the narcotics and the money was not an option. After tossing around a few different possibilities, we decided a diversion was necessary. After a brief discussion with the director of public works, he had an idea.

Skip R. 'Sea Legs' Cartwright. Director of Public Works. Skip was one of those people who seem to have nine lives. Known for pushing his luck around every corner, he never seemed to fall down except when he drank too much. He was notorious for showing up to drive the village snow plow when he was totally plowed himself. Skip had the appearance of a nineteenth-century sea captain with a big belly, salt-and-pepper hair and a beard to match. He looked and acted just like he'd stepped off an old whaling boat.

Skip suggested that he go into the building next door, plug a sewer drain and cause a backup. This would cause a backflow of raw sewage in the basement of the abandoned building and cause a big stink. Then we could swing by the firehouse and borrow a few of their large fans and self-contained breathing apparatus (SCBA). Coming from a guy known to have a serious alcohol problem, this plan sounded like drunken insanity.

Tommy spoke up. "Let me see if I got this right. Instead of running into the building and catching this guy we're going to make a big stink, then make him run out. Then we go into the building with self-contained breathing apparatus and decommission all the weapons and explosives." I said, "If you have a better plan, let's hear it." He paused for a minute, then said, "This goes against all the training." A date was set; we ran it by the lieutenant and the chief. Both of them shook their heads and said, "This better work."

We set up stakeouts at both ends of the street. Skip went to work in the building next door. Two plainclothes officers flipped over a manhole cover and set up some orange cones in the street in front of the abandoned building. It took about three hours before we could make out the stench. We were sure that if we could smell it, the drug dealer in the abandoned building must be suffering. Moments later we saw him run out the back of the building with a scarf over his face, coughing and eyes watering. Maverick and the takedown team at the rear of the building nabbed the drug dealer as he fled the stench in the building.

When we got into the building, we discovered several other obstacles and dangers; this guy had set up the building to be virtually impenetrable. Man-sized holes drilled in the floor revealed escape ropes that went all the way down to the basement. It took us about two and a half hours to decommission the weapons and explosives.

When I walked down into the basement I removed my SCBA mask. The stench was so bad I hurried out of the basement and slipped in a pile of sewage backflow. My feet were soaked and unbearably stinky. I'd have to ask for new duty shoes after this mission was over.

We gathered up and inventoried the narcotics, money and paraphernalia we'd found in the abandoned building and took them to the safe at the police station. I radioed Skip in the building next door and told him to open up the drain.

Tommy and I had a short discussion and debriefing at the police station. He said, "I think your idea was totally and completely crazy, but because everybody worked together we managed to pull it off.

I'm starting to find a lot of respect for you small-town cops."

Chapter 10

Being a police officer gives you the opportunity to see a person one day at their very best and, maybe a month or so later, see the same person at their very worst. This window of perspective produces a great deal of wisdom and insight into the human condition.

> *Roger Dorsey. A very well-known realtor around the area. To all outward appearances he had the looks of a movie star and the wealth to match. When he came into town he usually drove an ostentatious gold SUV and had Katie, his gorgeous trophy wife, riding in the front. Katie was always sparkling and smiling like the beauty queen she'd once been.*

The real estate company that bore Dorsey's family name had been established over a hundred years ago by his grandfather, and they had three generations' worth of wealth reinvested by the family. Some people in town were a bit resentful, or perhaps merely envious, and believed it was time for the Dorseys to give a little back to the community.

One Friday night around 11:00 I received a dispatch of a 911 call coming in from Highview Corners, the very wealthy neighborhood just north of town. Typically, the sheriff's department would take this one, but they were overloaded and had me cover their call. The call came in as a burglar alarm motion detector at the back of the house. I got on the radio and said I would be en route to Highview Corners.

I expected to see nobody on the property and no vehicles in the driveway but was pleasantly surprised to see the big gold SUV I recognized as having come through town about a week ago. After making my way to the back of the house I found a middle-aged woman, very beautiful, with a large cut on the top of her head. She was trying to break into the house. I said, "What's your name and do you know who lives in this house?"

She was visibly shaken and distraught. "I live here. My husband beat me up and locked me out. I'm Katie Dorsey." I said, "I need to see your driver's license." She collapsed on the ground, shaking and crying. I decided to call EMS. I knelt on the ground next to her and asked, "Where is your husband?" She asked if I knew him well, and I said no, but that we'd met once or twice. She said, "Roger is good at creating illusions."

I asked her again where Roger was, and she said he was probably at the country club. I asked where they were when he struck her in the head; she got very quiet and then started talking about how Roger's lawyer had a lot of guns and bad people working for him.

She was quiet for a moment and then started to recount what had happened earlier that night. "We went out to dinner at the steakhouse, then went over to the country club for drinks. Roger's lawyer showed up and started asking about the next deal. I accidentally said something to the lawyer about Roger's pet monkey. I forgot that Roger told me never to bring up the monkey; it was supposed to be a secret between us. Roger got very angry and said, "If I could afford to divorce you right now I would. I'm trying to figure out if it would be cheaper just to have you killed." She continued, "I knew I was in big trouble. He forcefully pulled me out of the country club, then pushed me into the Lincoln and drove out into the country. At Hickory Street and 32nd Avenue he stopped, grabbed my purse and threw it into the swamp, smashed my cell phone, and then picked up a bottle of champagne from the back seat and hit me over the top of my head with it. He warned me that if he sees me alive after this he's going to pay somebody to kill me. He said, "Consider this an instant divorce without assets." I walked through the fields about three and a half miles to get home, so I could get some clothes and call my mother to come and get me."

I asked her if something like this had ever happened before, and she said, "Yes, often. Roger has serious troubles." I asked, "Why did he get so upset about the pet monkey?" She replied, "If he ever lost a deal, the monkey would squeal." I told her that I didn't understand what she meant. She said that the monkey lived in a miniature house in the woods behind their home. "If Roger got upset about a deal, he would go pay the monkey a visit and kick it in the balls."

I could hear the fire truck and ambulance coming down the street. I decided to call Katie's mother so she could meet us at the hospital. In the emergency room, Katie told the doctor that she had a lot of bruises and marks and that she had been beaten on many occasions. She was completely terrified of Roger; she knew that she needed to leave him.

Chapter 11

At the Village Council meeting, most members of the village government were present.

> *Gail R. Nicholson. The assistant village manager, Gail had that 'angry teacher' look permanently etched on her face. I've met some crazy people that I wasn't afraid of, and some who totally scare me, and she was part of that second crowd. She was known for sitting at her desk and pounding on her calculator so hard that the keys seemed like they might shatter, with a look on her face like she wanted to strangle somebody.*

> *Chris S. Matheson. The village manager, Chris had that sleek, successful businessman look. Chris was the polar opposite of Gail, very peaceful and logical. He never seemed to get ruffled by anything, but he obsessed about every dollar in the village budget.*

> *Lori B. 'The Decorator' Lundgren. The police department secretary, Lori had a vibrant old lady look with eyes the color of steel. Lori was an excellent police secretary, always on top of her game, but she seemed overly concerned about flowers and things not being kept up at the village cemetery.*

At the meeting, a man from out of town said that he would like to hold "an event to recognize and celebrate people of German ancestry". Since it was late in the evening and everybody wanted to finish the meeting, they recognized his idea and asked him to put a proposal together. No one, at the time, was aware that he was the leader of a white supremacist group. The man went directly to the clerk, paid the fees and set a date for the event.

After the man had left the meeting, Gail Nicholson, assistant village manager, said, "I have a bad feeling about this event. It kind of sounds like a white supremacist rally. I've been hearing that they're happening more and more lately; we'd better get more information."

Chris Matheson, village manager, wondered aloud, "How much money could we make by having an additional festival this summer? This could bring in a lot of revenue."

Lori Lundgren said, "We'll need additional flowers and organizing in the parks and cemetery before we can have a beautiful festival. I'll take care of all of that."

At the next meeting, many people started asking questions about the event. Gail had been correct in her concern that the event was actually a white supremacist rally. The man seemed to enjoy answering people's questions with more questions, which irritated the members of the village council. They tabled the discussions and the proposed rally went into arbitration, where a state board listened to arguments. The arbitrators concluded that there were no laws forbidding what, by this time, everyone knew were white supremacists from having the rally in the center of the town on June 29th.

A plan for structure and security at the rally was set. Surprisingly, protesters of white supremacy would outnumber the rally members, and our job would be to protect the white supremacists from the protesters. A riot with thousands of people was possible. The biggest challenge was coming up with the money in the budget to pay for all the overtime. It was estimated that it would cost about 800 man-hours of labor to cover all the preparations, the rally, and the cleanup afterward. There would be three different law enforcement agencies necessary – state police, county sheriff and local police, including a few undercover officers and miscellaneous personnel. An enlarged, heavy-duty eight-foot fence with metal detectors, bomb-sniffing dogs and video surveillance were deemed necessary. At the planning meeting, the sheriff decided at the last minute to activate the mounted division, bringing another 20 officers with their horses and equipment. At times an air of paranoia came over the room. Very level-headed, logical people started to worry about all the details.

The village brought in a risk manager to study the situation and consulted with other towns that had had similar rallies. The risk manager looked at the plan and said that everything was in order.

On Saturday, June 29th – the day of the rally – the chief and the lieutenant held a meeting at the squad room. When I walked in, the energy was electric. Never were so many officers from so many departments present at a briefing. The chief started the briefing, then turned it over to the sheriff, who said, "We are prepared and ready for 95% of the contingencies today."

Shortly after the sheriff finished, Sergeant Larry Wallace took the podium. He reminded everyone of their assignments, that the mounted division was in charge, and that everyone was to defer to him on the radio for instructions. Everyone confirmed and went off to their duty stations.

The tactical plan was to set up a safety zone between the white supremacists and the protesters. The area outside the fence was reserved for the protesters and the zone inside the fence was the safety zone for the white supremacists. If we kept them separated there could be no violence. I couldn't help but think of that well-known line in the song "Come Out and Play" by The Offspring – "You gotta keep 'em separated" – and that line ran through my head all day.

The white supremacists' bus arrived right on time and we escorted them to the fenced-in area. They began their announcements and the rally was started. Everything was going well. I settled into a comfort zone and started to think everyone was making a big deal out of nothing.

A half-hour passed without much action. Then I saw a crowd of protesters marching up the street, much larger and much louder than expected. My brief estimate was that the protesters outnumbered the white supremacists two to one.

Now I was seeing the big picture; we were there to protect everyone, but the protesters had the numerical advantage. Within ten minutes the whole rally environment changed. I could see the anger on people's faces. Sergeant Wallace spoke up on the radio and said, "Everyone stay in your positions."

The white supremacists rushed out to meet the protesters, creating a large melee in the street. We managed to push the protesters back up on the curb. Just as things were getting out of hand, Larry rode up on his horse with the rest of the mounted division. Larry and the other deputies started screaming, "Here comes the tear gas." The sight of Big Larry up in the saddle, holding a tear gas rifle, was awesome.

Both sides of the rally took notice. The energy settled. Larry made eye contact with both leaders and they acknowledged his threat with the tear gas. The white supremacists backed down and moved back behind the fence. The protesters took that as a victory and backed up onto the curb. Both sides made some posturing motions toward the other. Things moved into a slow simmer mode. About an hour later the white supremacists announced the rally was over. They all got back on the bus and left.

Chapter 12

It was early October and the leaves were coming off the trees. I was working a day shift with my favorite partner, Maverick. He said, "Let's start the day off with a good meal." That sounded pretty good to me, so we hit the local diner and ordered some breakfast. Maverick said, "Hey Patty, do you think it's going to be busy today?" I said, "It's Sunday; probably no big calls today. I heard somewhere that bank robbers sleep in on Sundays. You know, the bank is closed." He laughed and said, "Where in the hell do you get your information? The ATM is always open." "Oh, yeah?", I retorted. "I'll let you have the call if someone is robbing the ATM. I take the call if the robber is pointing a gun at someone since I'm a better shot than you." I could almost see steam coming out of Maverick's ears and knew better than to say anything more.

The last time we'd been at the gun range qualifying, Maverick's gun had jammed, and I beat him by one point. His ego was still a little sore. This was the one and only time I shot better than he did. Typically, he shot about ten points higher than me over the past couple of years. The chief was the only person who consistently shot better at the range than Maverick.

Maverick changed the subject. "If we get a call to help a little old lady today I will let you have all the glory." I said, "You better stick to your word." As we finished eating, the chief and his wife walked in. He waved and told us to be careful out there. As we walked out of the diner Maverick said, "Let's split up the patrol today. You take the parks and I'll take the schools." I said, "You got a deal."

After making the rounds at the parks, I decided to stop by the firehouse and see some friends. By the time I got there, Maverick's cruiser was already parked in front of the firehouse. I walked in and said to Maverick, "Did you really drive by the schools before coming here?" He just laughed and replied, "Are you fucking crazy?" Maverick asked, "So how are the parks?" I said they were good. "Are all the gates unlocked and swung open?" I said yes. He laughed and said, "It's Sunday; all the schools are closed." I shook my head and muttered, "Asshole."

As we hung out with friends at the firehouse telling stories of past glory, a call came over the radio to check the welfare of an elderly woman. Maverick said this was his call, but I reminded him about the conversation at breakfast. Something about a little old lady? He reluctantly agreed and said, "I'll follow you over there and help."

When we arrived at the address we found a very old colonial house in disrepair. We walked around the back and it appeared that no one had driven the car in the driveway in many years. As Maverick sized up the scene, I called dispatch. The dispatcher told me that a 92-year-old woman named Lois lived there alone. Typically, Lois called her granddaughter every Tuesday and Saturday. The granddaughter had received no calls this week. She lived 300 miles away and she was concerned about her grandmother's health.

I communicated dispatch information to Maverick. We had a brief discussion, and he said, "I'm not comfortable using forcible entry; we don't have exigent circumstances." I asked, "In your humble opinion what would cause us to have exigent circumstances?" We walked around the front porch, knocking on the door and front window announcing, "Police department; please answer the door." I saw a cat in the window, and the cat appeared to be in distress, running and bouncing, making hissing noises. The cat even tried to pull the curtain back with its teeth to show us something. I said, "Maverick, I think Lois has suffered a medical emergency and is unable to come to the door." Maverick said, "Nonsense, I've had lots of calls like this. She's just gone away for the weekend and forgot to call her granddaughter."

We sat there for a minute discussing the proper course of action. I said, "Maverick, let's knock really hard on every door and window, front and sides of the house, and then let's wait quietly with our ears to the window to see if we can hear anybody calling for help."

Maverick said, "If that will get you to shut the fuck up and move on, let's get 'er done." Just then, firefighter Glen Rawlings stepped up onto the porch and asked what we were doing. I explained. He told us that the fire department had been there twice in the last month to help Lois up after she fell. As the three of us put our ears up to the front window, we could hear a faint cry for help. I looked at Maverick, and he looked at me in surprise.

Glen had put his size-12 boot to the front door and was kicking in the door to get in to help Lois. When we got to the kitchen and found her, she was in bad shape. She looked like she had been on the floor for the better part of two days.

She was dehydrated and very sick. She appeared to have a broken hip and other miscellaneous injuries. The pallor in her face showed that she was near death. I got on the radio and called fire rescue and an ambulance. The three of us knelt on the floor trying to stabilize her and make her more comfortable. We gave her water and coached her to hang on.

When the fire truck and ambulance arrived, I went outside to help bring in the gurney. We all worked together to get Lois on the backboard and into the ambulance.

We straightened up the house and took the cat to the neighbors' house. Next, we called the granddaughter to tell her what hospital her grandmother was being taken to and called a construction contractor to secure the door.

When we returned to the police station, Maverick told me, "This is your call; it's your job to write the report." I said, "Yes, my call and this time it was my idea that saved her life."

Chapter 13

It was the first week in March. It was cold, about 25 degrees out. Light snow was falling, the streets were slippery, and traffic was moving slowly. Earlier in the day I had been investigating some broken windows in the old paper mill. The driveway was covered in snow and unbeknownst to me, the kids who'd broken the window did it before the snow started to fall. As I drove up the driveway to the mill, I heard broken glass under the snow, slightly puncturing my right front tire. I decided to back out and head over to the public works department to see Skip and have the tire repaired.

When I arrived, Skip was sitting at his desk doing some paperwork. I mentioned that I'd been at the paper mill and ran over some glass under the snow. Skip laughed for a minute and said, "I never heard that one before – glass under the snow." He went on to say it would be late in the day before my cruiser would be fixed, so I'd better call for a ride. I got on the phone and called Maverick. "My cruiser is at the public works getting repaired; come get me." He growled into the phone that it would be 20 minutes.

In about 20 minutes, Maverick came by and picked me up. He said with a smile, "How did you fuck your cruiser up?" I started, "There was glass under…", then stopped and said, "Slow leak on the tire." He said, "Yeah, the tires on the cruisers are junk." "Looks like we'll be a two-man team in this car for the rest of the shift," I said. "Okay", he replied, "then you're buying lunch."

We swung by the diner, where Maverick ordered a steak with potatoes and corn. I opted for the fish with rice and green beans. As we spoke, I realized that we had not been called over to Prairie Township in a while. I said "Y'know, I wonder what's happening with the guys over in Prairie Township?" Maverick replied, "I don't know; it's been a couple of weeks since I've been over there."

We headed back to the office to finish some reports and do some paperwork. Shortly after we completed that, we received a dispatch. "We have a report of shots fired coming from the house across the street from 699 Jefferson Avenue in Prairie Township." Maverick gave me a very strange look and told me to grab the shotgun and get in the cruiser. As we were leaving, Maverick activated the lights and siren.

As we were heading over to Prairie Township, about ten minutes away, we received conflicting information over the dispatch radio. I told Maverick, "You better step down on that accelerator and get over there before somebody dies."

Coming up to town, we were approaching a yellow light. Maverick slowed down to about ten miles an hour. We checked all directions in the intersection, and all vehicles appeared to stop. As we approached the intersection, I heard the screech of tires just before there was a hard collision on the driver's side of the cruiser. I was in the passenger side and the impact threw my neck to the side. I blacked out.

The next thing I could remember, the cruiser was down in the ditch on the side next to the cemetery and Maverick was sitting in the driver's seat, stunned, with a fair amount of glass in the side of his face. Maverick was too shaken up to talk. I picked up the radio, called county dispatch and told him that we were out of service and to dispatch fire rescue to our location. All I remembered after that was waking up in the back of the ambulance on the way to the hospital. The paramedics told me that I had a neck injury and possibly a broken knee.

After a complete examination by the emergency room doctor, it turned out that I had a vertebra in my neck that was out of place but not fractured, and that my knee was bruised but the bones were all intact. A few moments later, the chief walked in and said he was glad to see that we were getting better.

The doctor turned to the chief and said, "I'm going to discharge both your officers to rest and recuperation at home." The chief told both of us that he would call in a couple days to check in with us.

After about a week off work, we were both climbing the walls, so Maverick and I went down to talk to the chief. As we sat in his office, we pleaded with him to let us return to work. He called the doctor at the hospital and explained the situation, and the doctor released us back to work.

After leaving the chief's office we walked out into the parking lot discussing the accident. I said, "Something like that could happen to anyone; we were just in the wrong place at the wrong time." Maverick nodded his head in agreement and said, "Let's put the situation behind us and get back to work."

Chapter 14

It was a beautiful Tuesday afternoon around 2:00. The sun was high in the sky, there was a light breeze out of the west, and the humidity was low – the perfect summer day. A 911 call came in for a two-car accident near 29th Street. I responded to the dispatch with fire, EMS and ambulance.

At the scene, we found that a large GMC 4-wheel drive truck, which appeared to have been going northbound on 29th Street, had struck a small subcompact Toyota, putting it over on its side and down into the ditch on the north side of the intersection. The GMC pickup truck was driven by a man in his early forties. He appeared to have small abrasions on his face from the airbag and was standing next to his truck shaking his head.

The Toyota that was down in the ditch on its side was occupied by two young women in their twenties. Both had significant, life-threatening injuries. The driver asked repeatedly, "Whose fault was the accident – did I hit the truck or did the truck hit me?" I asked her name and whether she had a purse in the car, so I could get her driver's license, as she was going in and out of consciousness. I could tell by the pallor in her face that she had life-threatening injuries. When we got to the passenger, she initially seemed to be less injured; but looking at the accident, it appeared that the truck had actually struck the passenger-side door, which should have given her substantially more impact injuries than the driver, leaving us with several questions. A crew of paramedics were dispatched to the driver of the truck, who refused assistance. We dispatched another set of paramedics for the women in the Toyota. The fire chief decided that we would extricate them from the vehicle using the Jaws of Life, so we started to cut the A, B and C pillars on the Toyota while other firefighters climbed into the car to stabilize the injured occupants. The driver's initial vital signs appeared to be bad but not critical, but the passenger's vital signs were now starting to decline, and we realized that we had perhaps a five to ten-minute window to get her out of the car and save her life.

One of the paramedics came over and advised me that the driver of the pickup truck had refused care but had a strong odor of alcohol on his breath. He suggested that I perform a field interview on him before he got away. I spoke to the driver and got his license, registration and proof of insurance. He was visibly nervous, asking a lot of questions about how bad the injuries were in the car. I told him that the fire department was doing everything they could. Just about then, a state police officer pulled up – Jake Chisel, the post commander.

Richard J. 'Jake' Chisel. State Police Post Commander. Only 29, he had risen rapidly through the ranks from state police trooper to post commander in just eight years. Jake could be high-strung, abrasive and aggressive when he was angry but was normally a soft-spoken guy at the office.

I asked the driver of the truck to stand by and went to explain the scene to Jake, who said, "Let me have the driver of the truck; you work the other side of the scene." As I was walking away, I saw him start the field sobriety tests. I assumed that the driver was intoxicated and would end up charged with drunk driving.

As I approached the Toyota, I saw the fire chief's face and recognized that he was really tense. When I got around to the passenger side of the Toyota they had the passenger on a backboard and firefighters were performing CPR. When they'd extricated her, she had gone into cardiac arrest. The driver of the car was just about ready to come out; she was in and out of consciousness, still mumbling about who caused the accident.

When they got her out and she saw her friend on her back with firefighters performing CPR, she began to cry, screaming, "Please tell me I didn't kill my friend!" As the firefighters were getting her onto the stretcher, I walked up slowly and mentioned that the guy driving the truck ran the stop sign and it appeared that he had been drinking. I knew this information was privileged and I was not supposed to communicate it at the scene, but I needed to relieve her conscience. Her eyes flooded with tears; she let out a big breath and said, "Make sure you arrest that guy."

As I glanced back across the road I saw the driver handcuffed and sitting in the back seat of the state trooper's cruiser. As he gazed out the window, his face was a mask of terror, pain, embarrassment and shock. Although the firefighters were doing CPR on the passenger of the vehicle, it was obvious that she was dead. The magnitude of what he had done, taking another person's life, had caught up with him.

When I returned to the station to write my report and do the accident diagram, I was still disturbed and emotionally stirred up. I needed to talk to another officer for a while and debrief in order to get my head together and write an effective report.

Chapter 15

Any time the number of people injured is larger than the number of rescue workers coming to help, the scene is considered a mass casualty incident. The actions and tactics of police, fire and EMS workers substantially change based on lack of resources.

One snowy December afternoon the weatherman predicted a large snowstorm with high winds, large snow accumulation, and a temperature of 28 degrees. As we sat around the firehouse listening to the weather report, the captain of the firehouse said, "Let's go double-check the truck and make sure we've got everything ready; you're probably going to have a number of calls today." Similar scenes were unfolding with the hospital emergency room staff and the paramedics' helicopter crew.

The first call of the afternoon came in around 2:00. We went out to the interstate and found a simple one-car accident where a car had slid off the road in the snow. We removed the patient, got him stabilized, and sent him to the hospital in an ambulance. We returned to the firehouse thinking this was going to be easy.

A little later, around 3:30, we received a report that an 18-wheel semi-truck had rolled over; several cars were involved, and interstate traffic was shut down in both directions. When we arrived on the scene, the semi-truck and three other vehicles were on fire. We had a total of 14 vehicles and 29 patients to handle. The captain got on the radio, declaring the scene a mass casualty incident, while we called for mutual aid from other fire departments in the surrounding area. The deputy fire chief and other captains from around the area also responded, bringing the number of rescue personnel to about 20. Six of the vehicles required extrication of the occupants, and in the space of 45 minutes we had three patients declared D.O.A.

One police officer and two firefighters were injured on the scene, adding to the already high number of patients that needed to be transported to the hospital. After overwhelming the local ambulance companies, the captain got on the radio and called for the chopper. It was only six miles from the accident scene to the hospital, but we had a shortage of ambulances. The captain instructed me, "Take some orange cones and set up a landing zone about 300 yards east on the expressway and place some flares on the roadway to help the helicopter." We radioed in the exact GPS coordinates and explained to the helicopter pilot the size of the landing zone.

Within about ten minutes we could hear the helicopter coming as we organized the patients on backboards, trying to keep them out of the weather by parking the rescue trucks to block the wind. Once the pilot had landed, he explained that they could take three patients per trip and that they would be running relay between the accident scene and hospital. After we got all the patients stabilized and transferred, we started to investigate the scene. We knew we'd be out there for hours mopping up hotspots, taking pictures and working with wrecker drivers to get the expressway opened up.

Chapter 16

The morning before Christmas Eve, around 11:00, I was on my way back from court. My cell phone rang, and I saw that it was Maverick calling. He said, "You better get back to the office." I asked why, and he said, "It's the chief. Appears to be having heart trouble. EMS is here, and they have him on a 12-lead electrocardiogram right now. The lieutenant is calling a meeting of all personnel."

By the time I got back, the ambulance had left, and everyone was talking in the squad room. Lieutenant Dan announced, "The chief appointed me temporary chief while he's out of commission. He is stable and in good condition but was having chest pain. Let's hope he's coming back soon after he receives the proper treatment for his heart. Maverick will assume the lieutenant position. I will be looking for volunteers for overtime; see the posting on the bulletin board. Does everyone understand their new assignments?" We all said that we did, and the meeting was dismissed. Maverick said, "C'mon, Patty, let's go grab some lunch." Over lunch, Maverick went on at length about how he had always dreamed of being chief and that, if the lieutenant went to work for another department, he was certain the chief would make Maverick the temporary chief. We started to dream out loud about what we would do with the department given the opportunity to make all the decisions; we would upgrade the cruisers, adjust shifts and get double coverage on weekends and holidays.

Chapter 17

A typical conversation during a stakeout goes something like this: Maverick asks me, "What are you doing after your shift?" I say, "I'm picking up my kids. How about you?" Maverick says, "I need to go run my kids up to Little League." After a long pause, Maverick then says, "We're stuck in this car for the next eight hours. What the fuck should we talk about?"

Eventually the conversation breaks into what we refer to as 'word bantering' or 'conversational shadow boxing'. It's the nature of a cop's competitiveness and aggressive disposition.

I ask Maverick, "Have you ever wondered why Socrates said, 'The only true wisdom is in knowing you know nothing' and 'The unexamined life is not worth living'?"

Maverick says, "Have you ever wondered how Tiger Woods was able to learn golf so young?"

I come back with, "Have you ever wondered why Plato said, 'Wise men speak because they have something to say; fools because they have to say something'?"

Ignoring my questions, Maverick says, "Have you ever wondered how Shoeless Joe Jackson was able to bat .408 average?"

I say to Maverick, "Have you ever wondered why the Hippocratic Oath came about?"

"Hypocritical Oath? What the hell is that?", asks Maverick. "More importantly, did you ever wonder how someone can bowl a 300-point game?"

"Mav, you ass, it's the Hippocratic Oath, not Hypocritical Oath," I say, laughing. "Have you ever wondered why Pythagoras tried to find a mutual harmony between real life and the practical aspects of philosophy?" I add, "And it isn't the shoes or the golf club or even the baseball bat. It's the dream and passion that live in the heart of the athlete that make a champion."

Maverick says, "Don't you have anything better to do with your life than to study philosophy?" I shake my head and reply, "Nope. I'm divorced and bored; besides, I like studying philosophy." Mav just stares at me and says, "You need a hobby. Or a woman."

Chapter 18

As I walked into the briefing room the tension was palpable. 'Red Knife' Murphy had broken out of the state prison. Most of the guys in the department were not old enough to remember this guy because when Murphy was in town, the chief was just a young traffic cop. He had been sentenced to 30 years to life for killing and robbing an elderly couple. His girlfriend Caroline had always said that he was at home with her that night, but eyewitness testimony and blood evidence tied him to the case. Whether or not he killed those people, he most definitely at least saw them dead and stole their belongings. He was caught with some of their family heirlooms a few days later.

The U.S. Marshals arrived at the station early in the morning. U.S. Marshal Davis said that they needed our assistance in arresting Murphy and getting him back to prison. Most likely he would be coming back to see Caroline. I was hoping I would be assigned to the takedown team with the U.S. Marshals, but no such luck. My assignment was a mid-day solo stakeout from the field behind Carol Casanova's house, a field that was also adjacent to Caroline's house. I figured I'd better make myself comfortable.

I checked out from the equipment room a camouflage tent, some sleeping bags and lounge chairs, face paint, camouflage clothes, large binoculars, water canteens and some rations. I made my way in an unmarked car, parked down on a two-track and hiked into the designated stakeout position behind Carol Casanova's house. I radioed to a patrol car. Stan was covering someone's day shift.

> *Stan B. Markowski. In his late thirties, Stan was a midnight shift cop. Big, mean and cold-hearted, he emanated an aura of ego, anger, hate and revenge. Stan was the type of guy who played hockey not to win, but for the pleasure of seeing blood and broken teeth on the ice. He chose to work midnight shift because it gave him plenty of time to watch ESPN and catch up on his favorite TV shows. In all fairness, Stan's attitude sucked but his police work was high-caliber.*

I asked Stan to swing by the yard to see if they could see me in the back of the house. Stan radioed back, "You're totally black ops." There I sat, waiting for instructions from the U.S. Marshals. I was supposed to contact them directly if I saw activity inside the house.

After sitting in stakeout mode behind the house for almost six hours, I saw Stan pull up on the dirt road behind the field. He flashed his flashlight and shouted, "Come out, your assignment is over." When I made it to Stan's cruiser, he gave me a quick briefing and explained that the takedown team caught up with Red Knife Murphy in the alley behind the tavern. He was under arrest and the case was over.

Chapter 19

As I spoke with the clerk at the gas station getting my coffee, he said that life was a series of tragedies with brief interludes of reflection. I was stunned by his beautiful articulation of philosophy. I had found a kindred spirit.

He went on to tell me that his father-in-law, an expert lumberjack, was cutting down a tree in his yard recently. He cut the tree on the correct side and planned for all contingencies, and after cutting the tree it began to fall just where he expected. At the last moment, the tree turned 45 degrees on the stump; simultaneously, the wind changed direction and the tree fell quickly and directly on top of him, killing him. "That's a fluke. I'm so sorry for your loss," I said. He replied, "Thanks. I know it was a fluke, but I'm still in shock." Then he asked, "You're a cop; did you get called to the scene?" I told him I hadn't been on that case but had heard about it from a friend on the fire department. It was truly a bizarre turn of events. The clerk agreed and told me to be careful out there.

As I walked out I thought maybe I should run my cruiser through the car wash. As I was exiting the car wash I saw Maverick drive by. I knew by listening to the radio where he was headed and decided to follow.

When I got to the scene I said to Maverick, "I'm not jumping your call." Still, Maverick was pissed. I said to him, "Chill out and quit being an asshole; this is a multi-car accident and I know you hate to fill out the UD-10 form. I only came by to give you a hand. If you tell me to clear the scene I will do that immediately." Maverick looked perplexed for a minute, then mumbled, "Oh. You want me to work the accident and you're going to do my paperwork. That's almost too good to believe."

We both put on reflective vests and started to investigate the scene. I took the pictures and filled out the paperwork as Maverick directed the rescue workers and the wrecker driver. I looked up from the clipboard a few times and saw Maverick's face; he wore a shit-eating grin and looked to be in his element. After we finished the scene and got the boulevard opened back up to traffic, Maverick said, "Thanks for your help. I'll meet you back at the office."

I beat Maverick back to the police station and had almost all the paperwork done as he walked through the door. I raised my finger up and waved it in his face and said, "Where the hell have you been?" He didn't take kindly to the gesture but told me he'd had to run down to the hospital to get the rest of the statement from the driver of the second vehicle. I said, "Oh, that makes sense; yeah, that guy was barely able to talk at the scene. So, you waited for him to settle down at the hospital and then took the rest of his statement? My apologies." He said, "Let's see the paperwork. I want to see if you got all this shit right; if not, you're buying me dinner." After reviewing all the paperwork, Maverick said, "Every so often you have a good idea." I retorted, "More often than you. So I guess you're buying me dinner instead."

Chapter 20

I was just finishing a traffic stop on Jacobson Avenue when my cell phone rang. It was Maverick saying, "I need you to get over to my location as soon as possible."

When I arrived on the scene Maverick was talking to some county road commission workers. He walked up from the ditch and said they were working on the water main near the side of the road when the bucket on the backhoe struck something in the ground, and they want us to start an investigation. I asked what the backhoe had struck, and he said, "It appears to be human remains, possibly a middle-aged female." "Shit. Seriously?" I replied. Maverick shrugged, clearly shaken by the discovery.

I headed back to the trunk of my cruiser and got out the police tape. I set up the crime scene area by mounting the tape to the surrounding trees, then grabbed my camera and started to take pictures. Maverick briefed the county road commission workers and told them they should call their supervisor and end their work at this site until further notice, as it was now officially a crime scene. I saw Maverick make a call to the chief and assume a posture that was reminiscent of the last time I'd seen him completely stressed out. He hated to work homicides. He still had scars from the last homicide cases.

As we stood by the cruiser, I asked Maverick, "Remember that missing persons report we took about three months ago? I think the last name was Saban; the human remains would fit a similar profile of that missing persons report. Wasn't the village doing a sewer extension around here about three months ago?"

Maverick commented, "That's some pretty good police work; it appears you have a bulletproof memory. You're pretty good at tying loose ends together. I'm not sure if that's the same woman but let's take some detailed pictures of the clothing at the scene and when we get back to the office let's pull the description of clothing last worn by the woman in the missing person's report."

Going on my hunch, it took very little detective work to find that the clothing in the previous police report matched that of the clothing worn by the deceased woman at the crime scene. I said to Maverick, "You know what that means – that crazy guy that killed his wife, you know the one, the school teacher – it appears that we're going to get to charge that son of a bitch." Maverick said, "Slow down – let's tie all the loose ends together and get the lieutenant and chief to look at this case. We still have to wait for the coroner to make his determination on the cause of death. Let's put together a file with all the leads and all the information and hand it over to the lieutenant. I agree with you; it's probably the same woman but we need to nail down every single detail before we fill out a charging request."

At the end of the shift I said to Maverick, “It's been a pretty stressful day. Wanna go down to the gym and work out? Maybe we can let go of a little of this stress.” Later at the gym, we found a private area to talk. I told him, “I believe you and I might have solved one of the best cold cases the department has ever had. Who knows, maybe you'll get promoted.” Maverick reluctantly said, “I probably never would have tied the two cases together. Your observation was brilliant. I hate to admit it, but you got me on that one.”

About two and a half weeks later, I walked into the squad room and looked in my mailbox. The chief had sent a form letter to both Maverick and me stating that we had solved the case and that the prosecutor was going to proceed with murder charges against the husband. The chief went on to say that Mary Saban's family had been in to personally thank him for bringing justice to their family.

Chapter 21

Maverick and I were dispatched to a call – trouble with a subject. Upon responding to the scene, we found we were dealing with a person who was well-known around the village, Lizzie Borden. Yeah, that was really her name.

Maverick and I liked to joke that with that name, she never had a chance. Lizzie was a person of limited intellectual capacity. She did not meet the criteria for a diagnosis of mental retardation, but she did fit into the category of a protected person. Knowing this about her made it much easier to determine the proper course of action. She told us that her neighbors were growing 'flowers'. She went on to explain, "Not the kind of flowers that you look at; the kind of flowers that you grind up and smoke." She said that these flowers had pointed leaves that made her believe that it was marijuana. This statement left us with a troubling issue – the possibly questionable word of a protected person versus the good of the community.

After Maverick and I left the scene we had a short discussion about Lizzie's complaint. Maverick said, "I've taken the same report from Lizzie multiple times and investigated the neighbors. They're not growing marijuana. They're jackasses who tease the poor woman relentlessly. This is her act of revenge."

Chapter 22

It was Saturday, July 27th, the day of the summer car festival. The festival was a 30-year tradition and one of the largest car festivals in the region. People brought classic street rods and exotic cars from over 200 miles away. We expected an additional 12,000 people to visit the village over the weekend. It was a huge source of revenue for the community, and all the businesses stocked up on supplies.

The chief and lieutenant had set up a yearly plan. Around the first week in June they would budget for manpower, equipment and resources to be set aside for the summer car festival. Additionally, we were bringing in 24 officers from the reserve division of the local sheriff's department. We would have traffic assignments, security assignments, arts and craft shows, and additional vendors that needed security. Even the local Secretary of State office would set up a temporary trailer office to meet the needs of the community.

At 8:00 meeting Saturday morning, the lieutenant paired me up with Todd Martin. Todd would be my duty partner for the day.

> *Todd Q. Martin. A cop in his early twenties, Todd was a rather nervous and jittery guy. He enjoyed chain smoking even though it was against department policy. Just about every chance he had, he could be found puffing on a cigarette. Todd was a young guy who had seen*

action in Afghanistan and had worked VIP security for a general in the Army. He had accomplished a lot in the first few years of his adult life.

Todd and I would be working as a team at Hickory Bridge Park. Knowing Todd and his insatiable appetite for cigarettes, we would need to tag-team the eight-hour shift and I'd have to give him additional breaks so that he could get away to the bathroom for a cigarette.

I had worked in the past with Todd on road patrol and knew him to be a good and dependable cop. I struck a compromise with him. I suggested that he work the west end of Hickory Bridge Park near the porta-potties and bathrooms so that he could slide off to grab a smoke anytime he wanted. I would work the east end of the park and we would check in with each other about every two hours. Todd said to me, "That sounds like a great idea. Don't tell anybody I'm smoking in the bathroom or porta-potties. I don't think it looks good." I promised him, "Your secret is safe with me."

About three hours into my shift the chief came on the radio and said, "All units, please move to Tactical Channel Five." I adjusted my radio to channel five and stood by for further instruction. The chief came on and stated that he was moving duty assignments; all units working the parks would be shifting to road patrol, and road patrol units would be shifting to the parks. He gave no explanation for why he did this, but I got on the radio and acknowledged the order. A few minutes later the lieutenant and Peter showed up at the park, saying it was time for them to take over. I said, "Gladly. We'll take the cruiser and take over road patrol. It'll be nice to have some air conditioning; it's getting hot out here." As I got in the car with Todd I said, "Make sure you roll down that window so I don't have to choke on your cigarettes all day." Todd smiled, made a few light coughing sounds, then looked over at me and called me 'Mr. Baby Lungs'.

As we drove around town on road patrol the traffic was heavy. Todd said, "I know we need to focus on road patrol now, but wouldn't it be great if we got a felony drug bust?" I replied, "Don't count on it. But that would liven things up, wouldn't it?" A few minutes later I looked up as we drove slowly by a car parked on the roadside. Smoke was rolling out the window. I said to Todd, "Looks like the inside of that car is on fire. Turn around now!" He pulled a U-turn. As we pulled up, people were bouncing around in the car; as we approached we could smell the strong, distinctive odor of marijuana. I said, "Hey, Todd, you got your wish."

The car was occupied by two young women and they were lost. The driver said, "We thought we were in Indiana. We saw Amish people in buggies." Struggling to keep a straight face, Todd advised her, "No, you're in southern Michigan. You're close, though." Her eyes were red, and her speech was slurred. She was so stoned that she slipped and said, "We're late for a delivery in Middlebury, Indiana." Todd looked at me and said, "Call for backup." I got on the radio and called Maverick.

We got the two young women out of the car, handcuffed them and sat them on the curb. The smoke was so thick we rolled down the window and waited for the air to clear to conduct the search. We found marijuana and a pipe on the seat. When we got around to the trunk we heard one of the women mumble to the other, "Oh, shit."

We opened the trunk to find a bale of marijuana and paraphernalia. Todd looked at me and said, "Looks like the dealer ain't gettin' his dope." I said, "Yeah, and these two are going to jail." Moments later, Maverick pulled up. "Hey, boneheads...you're on road patrol, not Narcotics." I said, "I know. We saw the car on the side of the road and it appeared to be on fire, but it turned out it was just full of marijuana smoke. Once the smoke cleared so we could see, we found drugs on the seat and a large quantity of it in the trunk." Maverick said, "Is this my bust or yours?" "Sorry," I told Maverick. "It's Todd's case."

Maverick said, "I'll process the narcotics and you two process the prisoners, okay?" I read the passenger her Miranda rights and she asked for a lawyer. Todd Mirandized the driver and, like her friend had, she also asked for a lawyer.

Shortly after we finished taking pictures and statements, the county sheriff's department narcotics detectives showed up. After we gave them a brief summary, the lead detective told us to transport the two prisoners to the county jail and said that they would take over the investigation so we could get back to road patrol for the car festival.

Todd and I transported and booked the two women into the county jail, then returned to the police station to fill out a few reports and meet up with Maverick. I told Maverick, "It was all Todd's fault. He was wishing for a felony drug bust to liven things up when we're supposed to be focusing on traffic enforcement for the car festival." Maverick laughed and said, "Sure, you think he's that good that he can talk about getting a felony drug bust and produce one on the same day?" "No," I told Maverick, "Todd's not that good, but I am." Todd spoke up to say, "Hey, you fucknuts, since you're enjoying this so much, you finish the report. I'm going to go have a smoke."

Chapter 23

It was a Saturday morning and I had to process a domestic violence warrant. Getting a warrant for someone is complicated. First, you write a report and submit it to the prosecuting attorney. If he or she likes the report, it meets the letter of the law and the prosecutor feels the facts are accurate, he or she will send you down to meet with the magistrate.

The magistrate will often ask you to read the report and give an overview of your personal observations concerning the crime and the applicable law. The magistrate often has several questions that need to be satisfied in their mind before they're willing to sign the warrant.

After reading the report and showing the magistrate the photos of the woman's black eye and the man's scuffed up knuckles, she told me to stop. She picked up her gavel and started to wave it around in the air. She started in on a rant about "women who marry the first man they fall in love with instead of waiting for the one who respects them."

I nodded in agreement with the magistrate. She put the gavel down and picked up her pen. The moment she signed it, I thanked her and hurried out of the magistrate's chambers so I could go arrest the man who had committed the domestic violence. I couldn't help wondering whether it was something in the magistrate's life that had caused her to take the request for a warrant so personally, or just the constant parade of domestic violence cases taking their toll on her.

All day, even after my shift was over, I couldn't stop thinking about the woman who was the victim of domestic violence or about the magistrate's unusual reaction to my request for a warrant. Was this what our society was coming to? Was it so common for women to be abused? In my personal world, this was not something that happened. It bothered me to think that my little girl could grow up and have to face this type of situation. What if the photo of the woman with the black eye had been a photo of my daughter? The more I thought about it, the angrier I felt.

I went home after work, still angry, and changed my clothes. Uncharacteristically, I threw my clothes in the corner in my frustration that women get beaten and terrorized by men they love, and as a police officer I couldn't do anything about it until after it happened. I was frustrated that there was no way for me to prevent it from happening, and as the father of a little girl, I feared for her future safety. I resolved to do everything in my power to make sure my daughter grew up with a healthy sense of self-worth so that, God forbid, if anyone ever did abuse her, it would be the last time. I vowed to myself that she would grow up knowing that she's better than that, that she deserves more than that, and that she could always come to me if anyone mistreated her. If she were older I would have sat her down for a serious talk about domestic violence, but she was still so young.

I called the kids to say goodnight, like I always did, and I made sure to tell them both how special and wonderful they are. I told them they deserve the very best the world has to offer. I told them how much their daddy loves them, and that I think about them all the time, even when I'm not with them. Someday, when they're older, I would start having more serious talks with both of them; but for now, all I could do was make sure they knew they were loved.

Chapter 24

It was early on a Sunday morning, around 9:00 or so. The village was quiet, but as Maverick and I went out on road patrol we heard a motorcycle, possibly a Harley, revving its engine with loud pipes. We turned to go over a few blocks to see where the noise was coming from.

When we got to Lincoln Street, near the corner of Love Park, we saw a middle-aged man in his driveway with an assortment of tools, looking like he was repairing his motorcycle. We made a brief stop and talked to him, explaining that it was early Sunday morning and we could hear him revving the engine on his motorcycle from several blocks away, and that he was possibly disturbing the peace. Maverick went on to say, "We don't really want to make a big deal out of this; we just want you to run your engine later in the day or outside the village limits."

The owner of the motorcycle, a man named Walter, was precisely the type of guy most people would think of as a hard-ass outlaw biker. There are, of course, motorcycle clubs that consist of good-hearted, good-natured motorcycle enthusiasts who love the fun and adventure and are not in the motorcycle culture for any other reason. Walter was not one of them; he was the type who's in a motorcycle gang purely for illegal and illicit activities.

As I walked down the driveway and glanced back at Walter, he made eye contact with me in a way that left me with a slight chill of trepidation. My internal cop radar was on high alert.

As Maverick and I got back into the patrol car, he said, "Did you notice that Walter had three different motorcycle license plates strewn about on the driveway with his tools? I wonder if he is swapping plates of different motorcycles to disguise a stolen bike." "Mav, that's some really good police work on your part," I replied. "Let's keep an eye out for him today."

Later that day, Maverick and I were talking with one of the business owners at the farmer's market. He was concerned about security in his building; overnight there had been a few break-ins, and we were giving him a bit of advice on how to secure the building by setting up some security cameras he'd bought.

After finishing that assignment and writing a report at the police department, we walked out of the back of the police department. Between the houses on the next street over, I could see a motorcycle go by at a high rate of speed. The rumble of its pipes sounded familiar. I commented to Maverick that it might be Walter from that morning. Maverick said, "I don't think we could be that lucky, but let's jump in the cruiser and check it out."

The motorcycle rider ran through town, up and down streets and alleys, and eventually got away. I suggested that we go back to the house where we originally met Walter. When we went back to the house, we noticed that there was no longer a motorcycle in the driveway. Most of the tools were pushed up into the garage, and the garage door was partially shut.

We decided to go on about our patrol and consider it an unfounded complaint. While driving past the car wash, I glanced out the window and noticed a green Harley in one of the wash bays. I said to Maverick, "Turn around and go back to the car wash. I think I found our buddy Walter and his loud-ass Harley."

We pulled up behind him in the wash bay and activated the lights. As we got out of the cruiser, Walter approached us, aggressively shouting, "You have no right to harass me. I've done nothing wrong and you fucking cops are out to get me."

We got him to calm down and explained to him that we had seen a motorcycle like his racing about town and we just wanted to confirm that it wasn't him. When I requested Walter's driver's license, registration and proof of insurance, he said that the motorcycle was new to him and he didn't have it on him. Maverick ran the license plate through the computer and saw immediately that the plate belonged to a vintage Harley-Davidson, not this modern Harley-Davidson.

Walter picked up his cell phone and called his wife, knowing that he was in trouble. Within about five minutes, his wife showed up and tried to sweet-talk us, saying "Walter's a real good guy and he just has a funny thing for loud motorcycles."

I explained to her that he refused to give us his driver's license and we were going to have to arrest him.

"If you can get him to turn over his license, at this point all we really have is a motorcycle with an improper plate. We'll just write him a ticket and impound the bike. You could really help your husband by getting him to cooperate with us."

She did convince him to hand over his driver's license, but when we ran his license we saw that, although it was valid, he didn't have a motorcycle endorsement. I spoke with his wife and explained, "He's getting loud again, and we're going to have to arrest him for disturbing the peace but at this point, if you can get him to shut up, he's looking at only two traffic tickets. If not, it will be worse and more expensive. I suggest you see what you can do to talk him down."

As Maverick and I got back in the car he said, "Patty, I'll bet you lunch that Harley is stolen. You need to get the VIN number off the frame and run it through the LEIN database to see if that bike is stolen." I replied, "Mav, I'm not taking that sucker bet. I think it's stolen, too."

As I walked back toward the Harley to check the VIN number, I noticed a look in Walter's eyes that reminded me of a tiger right before it attacks its prey. His pupils were constricted, his eyes were darting around at a furious rate, and his hands were shaking. I squatted down next to the Harley and pulled out my notepad to copy down the VIN number. A moment later I saw a flash and felt a strong impact on my left temple. When I woke up on the cement floor of the car wash, I could hear scuffling and people screaming. I could hear Maverick fighting with Walter, and Walter's wife screaming, "Let him go! Let him go; he's a good guy!"

When I got up off the pavement I was seeing double and had blood running out of my left eye. I closed the left eye hoping to see better with just my right eye. I could see Maverick and Walter fighting near the trunk of the cruiser. Maverick was trying to handcuff him, but Walter was overpowering him. My only thought was that I needed to come up behind Walter and put an iron-arm hold on him so that Maverick could hit him with the Taser.

Previously, Maverick had told me, "If you ever hear me say "Code 86", that means get the fuck out of way because I'm taking aim. If you don't move out of the way you could get caught in the crossfire."

When I got near Walter I got my left arm around his body. I was really struggling with him; he was a strong, burly guy in the midst of an adrenaline surge. Maverick stepped back and was screaming but in the rush and noise of it all I couldn't really make out the words.

At the last moment, Maverick pushed me away, pulled out the Taser and hit Walter. As Walter fell, he knocked me back down on my right side and fell on top of me with the Taser darts still stuck into his chest. I could feel a little bit of electricity trickle from the back of his body into the front of mine; it was a weird sensation.

All I could think was that I wanted to get this fucker off of me and get up off the wet cement.

While I tried unsuccessfully to get up off the pavement, Maverick rolled Walter over and handcuffed him as his wife was screaming, "I think you killed my husband! I think you killed my husband! I'm gonna get you fucking cops."

Maverick collapsed on the ground next to me, looked over at me and said, "Your face is really fucked up. You better get on the radio, call fire rescue, and get the lieutenant over here for backup." I said, "I will if you'll get your ass up off the ground and keep an eye on Walter's wife. I wouldn't trust her as far as I could throw her."

Chapter 25

It was a little after 11:00 on a Saturday night when Maverick and I were dispatched to a suicide call at a local tavern. As we walked into the bar we made our way to the bartender, who stated that there was a regular customer who went by the name of Billy and he was having a bad day. He'd told the bartender that he was possibly ready to commit suicide. Sitting down with Billy in order to seem less intimidating, we told him he wasn't in trouble. I went on to tell Billy that people at the bar were concerned about his well-being, that we'd heard he might be thinking of harming himself, and that we were there to help him.

Billy was an older gentleman who had experienced a lot of instability and stress in his life. He was also abusing both alcohol and drugs and was emotionally unstable. Billy's chief complaint was that he was in love with a woman who came into the bar and drank with him on regular occasions, but he had heard that she was no longer interested in dating him. He kept saying, repeatedly, "I need to figure out if she's just mad at me or if it's totally over. If it's over with her, there's no point in going on." I explained to Billy that suicide was a permanent solution to a temporary problem. I tried to make him see that the peak of this emotional reaction would change with time. He kept repeating, "I'm not going to live without her; I can't live without her." I couldn't help noticing that, in the background, Eric

Clapton was singing "Cocaine", and I thought how appropriately inappropriate that was in this situation.

Maverick and I stepped away and had a quick discussion out of earshot of Billy. We both agreed that Billy was a risk to his own safety and that we would need to transport him to the hospital and have him seen by a psychologist on an emergency basis.

After getting Billy into the ambulance and sending him off to the hospital I had a brief discussion with the bartender. He told me that some of the people in the bar had come up with the idea of lying to Billy about his girlfriend.

I found myself getting angry as the bartender went on to say that the girlfriend was neither interested in breaking up, nor was she mad at Billy. She was simply out of town for the weekend and some of the regulars at the bar had thought it would be funny to play a sick joke on Billy.

While it was cruel of the regulars to get Billy all worked up and unfortunate that we'd had to send him off for a psych workup before we found out that it was all a mean 'joke', the fact remained that if Billy could get suicidal just because someone told him his girlfriend wanted to break up with him, he could benefit from the psychological evaluation and some mental health treatment.

I asked the bartender to point out the regulars who had been in on the prank. With Maverick following behind me wondering what I had in mind, I went up to the patrons and very sternly said, "Telling that poor guy that his girlfriend didn't want him anymore may not have been illegal, but it was cruel. Your sick little joke just cost the taxpayers a small fortune in police and EMT time as well as ambulance and hospital fees and kept us from doing other things to keep this little town of yours safe for you. If I wanted to, I'm sure I could find some law that you broke, but you're lucky; I'm just giving you a warning. Playing a stupid prank like that could have backfired on you in a big way; what if Billy had been carrying a gun and decided to kill the messenger? From now on, try to be decent human beings."

With that, I stalked out of the tavern with Maverick still trailing behind me, wondering what had set me off to the point that I'd lecture those cruel idiots about their behavior.

Chapter 26

I was out on patrol one day, heading south on Main Street, when I saw Maverick's car parked outside the house two doors from the end of the block. I was pretty sure that I knew who lived in this house; her name was Karen Smith, but many of the people in the village just referred to her as 'The Flower Lady'.

It was a small house on a simple lot, meticulously well-kept and maintained, but the yard was a wild, busy mix of flowers, bushes, plants, sculptures and horticultural tchotchkes such as garden gnomes and cutesy little signs and other objects. It was overkill in my opinion, but then again, my landscaping aesthetic was very minimalistic. To each his (or her) own, I guess.

Knowing that Maverick was an avid member of the Horticultural Society, I was not surprised to see that he had stopped by to talk to The Flower Lady and ask her about her plants. I pulled a U-turn at the end the block and pulled up in the driveway behind Maverick. I saw him and The Flower Lady pointing at some bushes and talking, and I stopped to absorb the true beauty and value of all the plants in her yard. Not being someone who knows much about gardening, I made some small talk and listened to them talk about different types of fertilizer, the varying nitrogen needs of different plants, pros and cons of different methods of watering, and all the hard work that goes into maintaining a beautiful lawn and flowers. Most of it was over my head.

Eventually I said to Maverick, “I think it's about time we go take a lunch break. If you want to run down to Subway, I’m buying.” Maverick smiled and said, “Well, if you’re buying, count me in.” He made parting conversation with The Flower Lady, and they both smiled as they shook hands. She thanked him for stopping by as we jumped in our cars and left for lunch.

When we sat down to eat, I said to Maverick, “The Flower Lady has one of the most beautiful yards I've ever seen but physically? She’s like five miles of rough road. Not to be mean, but a woman like that probably doesn't date much and has nothing else to do but spend time in the yard. If she spent some of that time on herself, maybe she’d find someone special.” Maverick said, “She's a beautiful person on the inside, but on the outside, yeah. She kinda looks like a man who's done hard work all his life out in the sun.” “Look at the upside, Mav,” I replied. “A woman like that is never gonna make your wife jealous if she finds out you been talking to her.” Maverick agreed, “You can say that again.”

Later in the day, we met up in the squad room at the police station. Maverick invited me to join him for a beer at the bar later, but I told him, “I’m really busy after work today. Maybe next time?”

Hours later, on my way home from softball practice, I noticed that Maverick’s fancy new Volvo was still at the bar. He wasn't the type of guy to go in and drink more than one or two, so I was wondering what the hell had gotten into him. I drove around the block and decided I'd stop in at the bar and say hi. I was stunned when I walked in and saw him sitting on a barstool right next to Karen, The Flower Lady I'd seen him with earlier in the day.

Maverick was dumbfounded when he saw me walk through the door; his cheeks and neck flushed bright red and he was clearly embarrassed. He popped up off the barstool, hurried over to me and said, "Patty, things aren't the way they probably look."

In a low voice, I said, "Look, Mav...it's none of my business if you've got something going on with her, but she just doesn't seem like your type. I mean, Helen's gorgeous and sweet. And a great cook, too. You hit the wife jackpot." He walked me farther away from Karen and said, "You're right, I did hit the wife jackpot. That's what this is all about. My wife's birthday is coming up and she loves flowers, and I've made arrangements for Karen to come over and put in a flower garden at my house to surprise Helen." I said, "Just don't forget the roses. Red ones and white ones; you know how Helen loves those."

He nodded and said, "That's in the plan. Please don't mention this to anybody, but I'm going to have Karen over to my house Thursday afternoon while Helen's out antiquing with her girlfriends. They're all in on it, too, and are going to keep Helen away all day while we put in the flower garden. I can't wait to see her face when she gets home and sees what Karen and I put together for her."

I told Maverick, "This all makes a lot more sense than when I thought for a split second that you were having an affair with The Flower Lady. Glad you got me on the same page; this is a beautiful thing you're doing for your wife. Your secret's safe with me. Let me know how it turns out, ok? Now I really do have to get home, so I'll see you tomorrow."

Chapter 27

I was driving by the firehouse mid-morning on October 30 before my shift began. The night before Halloween, known as Devil's Night, was unfailingly eventful, as the local kids would always try to outdo the mischief they'd gotten into the previous year. The fire chief was walking out and waved at me, so I stopped to say hello.

> *Thomas M. Douglas. In his late fifties, Tom had been fire chief for more than 20 years. He'd done a wonderful job with the small rural fire department, changing it from a ragtag, backward fire department to a much more professional organization that was respected by the community. The previous fire chief had been an ineffective leader and had lost his way, lacking ethics and principles, and had been dragged out kicking and screaming. It was not an ideal situation to inherit, but Tom had taken it on and turned the department around. Tom, and the fire department, were highly regarded in the village and by other area fire departments.*

Tom and I made small talk for a few minutes, and he mentioned that last year on Devil's Night we'd had six dumpster fires. "I've got an idea." I said. "Let's give those kids a surprise. Let's take the fire truck around town today and douse all the garbage in the large dumpsters. He laughed, "Joe, I love it. Soggy garbage doesn't burn. Let's do it! But we need to get it done before the kids get out of school and see what we're doing, or they'll just come up with some other stupid stunt for tonight."

We put together two crews, one doing the south side of town and the other doing the north side. It only took about three hours to hit all the major businesses in town. I asked Tom, "How many firefighters have you got on duty tonight?" He said he had 12 scheduled for the night and should have everything covered. Around dark, when the Devil's Night hijinks usually began, I was on patrol, monitoring police and fire channels on the radio. As the night went on, I chuckled to myself thinking of all the frustrated kids trying in vain to start dumpster fires; it was one of their preferred pranks because dumpster fires were self-contained and, therefore, relatively unlikely to get any of the kids in serious trouble.

Chapter 28

It was around 7:00 on a Friday evening when Lieutenant Dan asked me to organize a file on people with outstanding warrants. He asked that I organize it with the oldest warrants in the front and the most recent warrants in the back. He told me, "We have some really old warrants. The court called and suggested we put a team together to start serving warrants. They must be running out of things to do. The chief is going to prioritize the serving of all warrants going forward."

Early the next morning I sat down with Maverick to explain what the lieutenant had said. I told him, "I'd love to work together to serve some of these old warrants." Maverick agreed, and we started looking through the file and organizing them as the lieutenant had instructed. I found a warrant with a name I recognized. "Do you remember the time we arrested Willie Falcon?", I asked. Maverick said, "Yeah, I see him in the skate park all the time." I said, "Then let's go pick him up. I'll bet you that Willie's gonna be there today. Why don't we swing by the skate park, and if we don't see him there, we can go by his mother's house and try to pick him up."

When we got to the skate park we asked a few kids if they'd seen Willie. They told us that he'd been there earlier but had gone home to have some lunch.

Maverick and I arrived at Willie's mother's house. As we picked our way around the beer cans and beat-up children's toys cluttering the front walk, I muttered to Maverick, "I don't have a good feeling about this one." He told me to quit being a crybaby and knocked on the door. Willie's mother opened the door and let us into the front hallway. We showed her the warrant for her son's arrest; it was clearly the first she'd heard about it. With her voice shaking and tears in her eyes, she asked, "How much will it cost me to bail him out?"

Maverick told her, "This time it's a felony drug warrant and he's gonna need to be arraigned by the judge." She started wailing, "No, you can't take my son away," as she tried to push us out of the entryway and slam the door. Maverick gave the door a moderate push. There was a loud noise, and we heard her hit the floor and loudly start to cry. When we got back into the house we realized that she had been stalling us to let her son get away.

We determined that Willie's mother had an injured wrist and a few scrapes and bumps. I called fire rescue to bring an ambulance for her. Maverick got on the phone to the chief to explain the situation. The chief said to Maverick, "I know the woman you're talking about; I also have a bad history with her. She's not one of our more upstanding citizens. I'm sorry to hear she is hurt, but I suspect she's exaggerating her wrist injury; still, make sure she gets to the hospital and gets treated. Make a very detailed report so I can investigate the matter."

Maverick and I returned to the station and had a short discussion with the lieutenant. After reviewing the events and our handling of the case, the lieutenant told us about Willie's mother's long and difficult history with the police.

After finishing reports, we went back on road patrol. Maverick worried, "I know we followed all the proper procedures and didn't do anything against the law, but I also wonder if the chief's investigation will yield the same results. After what the lieutenant told us, I have a bad feeling about this." I told Maverick that I had the same feeling.

A few days later the chief called Maverick and me to a meeting in his office. We went over the report of what had happened with Willie's mother and gave him a verbal statement. He told us, "I believe you followed all the procedures. Unfortunately, I also have a bad history with this woman, and now she's complained about your treatment of her. Therefore, I have no choice but to turn this investigation over to Internal Affairs at the sheriff's department. Please contact Captain Richards at the sheriff's department. He will oversee this investigation. I'm sorry, guys. I don't believe her, but my hands are tied."

> *Captain Red K. Richards. In his late sixties, Red was in charge of Internal Affairs at the local sheriff's department. Red had been in the police department his entire professional life, working his way up from traffic cop to captain at the sheriff's department through a lot of hard work. That he was in the Office of Internal Affairs meant that he was a man whom a lot of people trusted and that he had earned the respect of his peers. He looked like a distinguished old man, and it was obvious his life had been full of stress, difficulty and disappointment. It was readily apparent by glancing at his face. His long,*

misshapen nose was evidence that he had seen some combat on the streets in the earlier years of his career.

Maverick called me the next day. "Isn't this fucking lovely, our little mishap trying to serve a simple warrant got both of us under investigation by Internal Affairs. For nothing! I told Helen about it last night, but I wish I hadn't because she's a wreck. You'd think that the chief could investigate this, see what happened, then exonerate us, but because of all these fucked-up circumstances, we have Captain Richards looking into the matter. The whole situation has me unsettled even though I'm positive we followed all the procedures and did nothing wrong."

About three weeks later, Captain Richards sent a letter to the chief. The letter stated that the warrant Maverick and I had been trying to serve was valid, that our entry was lawful, and that the injuries sustained by Willie's mother were the result of her obstructing officers serving a warrant. She had no legal right to block entry.

The letter concluded, "Your two officers are exonerated of any wrongdoing in this matter, and their service records should reflect this exoneration."

Chapter 29

There had been many 4th of July parades in the village. It was a tradition that went back more than 50 years. A lot of time and energy went into planning the 4th of July parade; more than 25 administrators and community leaders met every year to produce the master plan.

Ours was the largest 4th of July parade in the area; people came from over 50 miles away to our tiny village to see the parade. Nothing in the area even came close to our parade. It was not unusual to have 10,000 people show up.

In late June I was in a meeting trying to tie up the last-minute details for the parade. Some of the community leaders were concerned about security and parking at the parade. Sergeant Larry Wallace of the sheriff's department's Mounted Division stood up to say that the Mounted Division needed to go first this year. Last year there had been some sort of trouble with the horses. The chief spoke up and said, "Larry, I think that's a good idea. People want to see the horses and we don't want the horses tired and spooked this year."

Sergeant Wallace added the horses, the police, fire department, VFW and the rest. The chief and the village manager said, "So noted," and committed to making it happen.

After the meeting, Maverick and I went out on patrol and were talking about the 4th of July parade plan. I said, "Go figure...the one and only Larry 'Larger than Life' Wallace will be leading the parade." "Did you think the chief was going to pick you?" asked Maverick. I said,

"No. You're the guy who deserves to be at the front." He commented, "I will be right behind the horses and you; the lieutenant will be following me; that's all that matters to me."

After the meeting, the chief and lieutenant took me aside. The chief asked, "Have we ever told you about this character we have here in town named Daren David Taylor, AKA 'Mr. DDT'?" He's a guy in his mid-twenties who is suffering from severe mental illness. He's been in and out of mental institutions most of his adult life and we've had a few tips from the community that he got hold of a stolen gun and is off his medication."

They provided me with a photo and his last known address and told me to be on the lookout, considering this subject to be armed, dangerous and mentally unstable. I thought, "I'll probably never see this guy. He's probably in hideout mode." When I talked about it to Maverick, he said that Darren was actually an admirable character when he is off the street drugs, on appropriate prescribed medication and in therapy.

Maverick also mentioned that when Darren is on street drugs, his M.O. is to walk the streets, scaring and threatening people by waving a gun in the air. He's never done any serious time in jail because of his 'mentally ill' status with the court.

After finishing up some reports at the station, I went out on patrol. I went down to the south end of town and drove by Darren's last known address. The house appeared to be abandoned and the yard was filled with blight. I thought no one was living there.

The 4th of July fell on a Saturday, and the chief called all officers in to meet that morning at 7:00. He had a master plan on the chalkboard in the squad room. We all grabbed coffee and doughnuts and took our seats.

He called the meeting to order and went over the details. The parade would form in the lot in front on the middle school, then proceed through town down Main Street, then south on Rose Street, and would end at the parking lot next to the firehouse.

The chief barked, "Do you all know your duty assignments? Do you understand the timeline?" We all looked straight forward and said, "Yes, sir."

Maverick and I headed to the car wash at the service station. We grabbed a snack and I said, "If we get a call on the radio during the parade get the fuck out of my way. I'm the duty car this morning." "Ok," he said," I'll make room for you to bug out if a call comes over the radio."

After finishing all details and equipment it was 10:30, so we headed over to the middle school parking lot. There were a lot of people there, but we found our spot and waited our turn. Maverick and I spoke with some of the deputies of the Mounted Division, and they were saying that they hoped nothing would spook the horses this year, because last year was a disaster. I said, "This year all of you are going first and Larry is going to take the lead, so hopefully it will go according to plan." Many of the deputies in the Mounted Division were relieved about that. Larry had a take-charge personality and an almost magical touch with the horses.

As we all made final preparations to take off on the parade route, the chief stopped by in his cruiser and told Maverick and me, "As long as you follow the master plan we won't have any trouble this year. Just make sure you follow the master plan and call me on the radio if there are going to be any changes or delays." Maverick and I returned a simultaneous, "Yes, sir."

As the chief pulled out of the middle school parking lot I poked my right elbow into Maverick's ribs and said, "Let me go first; you can be second and no one else will notice." Maverick said, "The chief just said two minutes ago that we have to follow the master plan, so get in your cruiser and follow me."

As we pulled out of the middle school onto Main Street, the horses looked so beautiful. They were walking at about 4 miles per hour, just as the master plan called for. Many of the citizens of the community, as well as visitors, lined up on both sidewalks. People were smiling, laughing and clapping; it all felt very magical. I had been in parades before, but this was a new experience for me. For some reason, this parade seemed much more special and much more beautiful and festive.

As we turned south onto Rose Street, I saw the village manager standing on the corner with his wife in the same place as last year. He had a look on his face of complete satisfaction, a wonderful thing to see and a change from his usual grumpy, angry look.

The chief was standing with his wife on the next block down. He had a very peaceful, yet stern look on his face and appeared to be enjoying the parade. As we made it down to the sixth block of Rose Street, I knew we would be turning left into the parking lot next to the firehouse.

When I was looking forward, I noticed that Larry and the mounted division were approaching the corner by the firehouse. Everything was going wonderfully, and

I was thinking that this year there weren't going to be any problems with horses. I heard Maverick on the radio say something garbled, but I really couldn't make out the words. The next thing I knew, a teenage boy with a gun was moving off the curb and out into the street. It was hard to see who he was. He was holding a pistol in the low ready position, which caused Maverick to get back on the radio and call for the parade to stop.

I was having trouble seeing around all the horses. Suddenly everything had turned chaotic. Maverick was in the car ahead of me; he slammed on the brakes and got back on the radio again, screaming "gun". It appeared that the suspect was running out to take aim at Larry on his horse. Just then Maverick stepped on the brake, slamming his cruiser into park and jumping out. I sensed that the smart thing to do was to slam on the brakes and jump out to see what happened. As I got out of the car I saw Maverick running in front of his cruiser, drawing his service weapon and screaming someone's name. I started to move to my left. I could see the suspect and his weapon; it appeared to be DDT, but I wasn't sure. I saw the suspect lunge out into the street and try to shoot Larry, who was up on his horse.

The bullet struck the side of the horse's neck, causing it to rear up and throw Larry right off the horse's back as he was unholstering his gun. Larry landed on the back of his neck. Maverick was screaming at the suspect, trying to draw his fire off Larry. The suspect stopped for a moment, turned 40 degrees and took aim at Maverick. I saw Maverick take aim, but I could tell he was afraid of crossfire. Maverick was screaming frantically; I heard, "Darren, put the gun down or I'm going to have to shoot you." My suspicion that the suspect was DDT had been correct. Maverick was unable to get off a shot toward Darren without striking innocent civilians watching the parade and running for cover. As I made it to the front of my cruiser and the back of Maverick's, I could see Darren get a second shot off, hitting Maverick in the right hip. Maverick was charging at Darren, trying to tackle him and take the gun away. As I was about 20 feet behind him, Darren got off a third shot, which struck Maverick in the foot.

As Maverick got his right hand onto the barrel of the pistol and was trying to push the pistol down into the ground while trying to overpower Darren, the fourth shot went off, hitting Maverick in the left knee and knocking him to the ground.

Somehow in the struggle, Darren maintained his grip on the pistol. Maverick was down at his feet and was in bad shape. Darren turned back 40 degrees and started to take a second shot at Larry on the ground. Larry was flat on his back; the horse was on top of Larry's legs thrashing and convulsing. Larry was injured badly and screaming, "Get this fucking horse off me." Members of the Mounted Division and their horses were spooked by the gunshots and running in all directions, unable to help Larry.

I wasn't exactly sure what to do but I thought I would follow Maverick's lead. I screamed at Darren, trying to draw fire away from Larry. I started to charge Darren and was less than ten feet away when Darren turned back again 40 degrees and got off one shot, striking me in the right arm. Next, I was at point blank range and was struggling with Darren, trying to take the gun away from him. Somehow the gun went off and the next shot struck me right in the center of my chest.

I knew my bulletproof vest would probably stop the bullet, but it felt like somebody had hit me in the chest with a sledgehammer, knocking the wind out of me. My eyes started to blur, and I tried to take a deep breath but couldn't breathe. I fell straight back onto the pavement. Looking straight up at the sky, I noticed it was a beautiful day. Out of the corner of my eye, I could see the lieutenant charging up to Darren from behind, knocking him to the ground and removing the gun from Darren's hand. I tried to get some clarity, but things had happened so fast; one moment everything was great, then just seconds later I was shot and lying in the street.

I was sure Maverick was on the ground about 15 feet from me, bleeding out. When I looked in the other direction, some of the Mounted Division were trying to get the horse off Larry, who was lying in the street, bleeding. I tried again to take a deep breath but was unable to get any air in. I sensed that this was probably the end of my life. Slowly, the light started to fade away and I was gone.

The next thing I knew, I woke up in a bed. I opened my eyes but couldn't see very well. I decided to try to breathe. The last thing I could remember was being in a gunfight and I'd been shot in the chest and couldn't breathe. Was I alive or was I dead? I couldn't tell, but I didn't really like either option.

When I tried to breathe the pain was intense. I thought, "Pain is good; that probably means I'm alive." I could feel that my right arm was in a brace. I tried to move my left arm. It was attached to my body and appeared to be working. Slowly I moved my left hand up over my chest, not really wanting to know if there was a hole in my chest. When it got there, I could feel a lot of bruising but no hole in my chest. I started to feel relieved. "Shot in the arm, I can handle that," I thought. I was glad I'd put on the damn bullet proof vest. My next thought was that maybe I was just dreaming. I decided to take more deep breaths. I was sure I knew this smell; it was the distinctive smell of a hospital.

Just then, a nurse walked in, stopped short and said, "Oh, my. You're back! The doctor is going to want to know about this right away." I said, "Wait!" but she ran out the door.

A moment later the doctor walked in and introduced himself. "We didn't expect you back to consciousness today. We have you on a lot of sedatives. We expected you'd be out for the next three to five days." The doctor said, "Let me start by telling you that my number one goal is to not stress you. You have some swelling of the pericardial tissue of your heart, which is like a sac around the heart. This is no trivial matter. We've done several diagnostic tests, and fortunately there are no tears in the tissue, but the tissue is swollen and putting pressure on your heart. The ideal treatment for you is to keep you sedated to keep you from having any emotional pressure. This course of treatment will speed the healing and reduce the swelling of the tissue around your heart. I'll tell you this – I've seen injuries like yours only a couple of times in my 30 years of practicing medicine. Most people with an injury like yours don't survive. You're very lucky to be alive. You must have a guardian angel."

"I've conferred with other doctors in the hospital about your condition, and many of them said it's a touch-and-go situation. I wish I could put your mind at ease and tell you that you're out of the woods, but with an injury like this we have to err on the side of caution and keep you sedated."

I asked the doctor to explain to me what happened. "The chart states that you were involved in a gunfight, that you're a member of a local police department and had been shot in the line of duty." I asked about my friends, my fellow officers who were involved, but the doctor said he had no details. I said, "Are any of my family members here?" He said, "Yes, you have family members here, and I can let you meet with them briefly but then I'm going to need to put you back under sedation until your pericardial swelling is diminished." "How long will that take?", I asked. The doctor replied, "It's hard to say. We'll need to keep you sedated for an undetermined period, until your heart is no longer in danger. Just know that we're doing absolutely everything we can to get you through this."

My kids walked in, tentatively, with tears streaming down their faces. They said, "We thought you were in a coma. We're so glad you woke up." As I started to ask them questions, the nurse walked in with an IV bag and started to connect it to the IV pump. I said to the nurse, "Please wait," but she mumbled, "Sorry, doctor's orders". I said, "I love you kids," and then I saw the light in the room fade. I couldn't speak. I was out.

Chapter 30

When I woke up again everything was a blur and my mind was fuzzy. The only thing I knew was that I was still in the hospital. I took inventory. Let's see – I'm alive? I must be, because I was still in pain, although much less than before. I was shot? Yeah, now it was coming back. I'd been shot in the chest. I sent up a little prayer of thanks to God and the taxpayers for the bulletproof vest. Without it, I would have died in the street. My arm was still in the brace, so I couldn't have been out all that long. I remembered a doctor telling me he was going to put me in a coma, so my heart could recover. Was it better? Waking up like this – did that mean I was going to make it? I could breathe more easily. Where is everybody? Much like the time before, I was not sure if I should raise my hand up to see if there was a hole in my chest. I felt like screaming but was unable to muster up the energy. I finally did get my free hand up to my chest, and everything seemed intact. At least there was no hole in my chest. What the fuck happened to me?

After what seemed like hours, a nurse finally walked in. I asked her, "Where the hell am I?" in a voice gravelly from disuse. Startled, she looked at me like I was a ghost, then grinned excitedly. "Welcome back," she said. "Let me go tell the doctor you're awake." I asked in my gravelly voice, "Where the hell am I and how long have I been here?" "Let me get the doctor so he can answer your questions," she said as she hurried out of the room. "No, wait!" I said, but she was already gone.

A rather tall, very large doctor walked in. He said, "Glad to finally meet you. My name is Dr. Schmidt. I'm a hospitalist, which means I manage your care in the hospital and bring in other specialists as needed." He asked me my name and birthdate, and then asked, "Can you tell me what today's date is?" I said, "Last I knew it was the 4th of July, but I remember another doctor telling me I would be sedated for a few days." "Well, you've been out for a while. A week and a half," said Dr. Schmidt. "Your chart says you had a blunt force trauma to the sternum, causing acute cardiac injury. You were put in a medically-induced coma to allow for recovery." Dr. Schmidt went on to say, "We tried to pull you out of the medically-induced coma once it was no longer necessary for cardiac purposes, but your brain stayed in a state of coma for a few extra days. I'm happy to see that you're back and lucid."

I spoke angrily to the doctor, "I really need you to tell me what the date is today." He said, "The date is July 15th, so you've been here for 11 days." Dr. Schmidt went on to say, "It's very common for people who've had an injury like yours and been sick for a long time to have a lot of anger and frustration they need to work through, especially when a coma is involved. We have counselors here to help you." I said, "There's no way it's July 15th. The way I remember it, I was working for the police department and I was involved in a shooting at the 4th of July parade. I woke up here in the hospital once before and another doctor told me he needed to keep me sedated for a few days. How can this be?"

Dr. Schmidt told me, "As I mentioned, we tried to bring you out of the medically-induced coma after a week, once the danger to your heart was resolving. Your brain, however, had other ideas and you remained in the coma for another four days. We've kept you here rather than sending you to a rehab hospital while the neurologists tried to determine the cause of the extended coma." With a laugh, he said, "Maybe you were just tired? I'm not noticing any neurological deficits as we've been talking, but I'm going to get one of the neurologists in here to give you a full workup now that you're awake, just to be on the safe side."

Dr. Schmidt said, "We've got someone coming in shortly to do an EEG to look at your brain function." Just then, a gorgeous EEG tech walked in pushing a machine. She and Dr. Schmidt bantered with each other and with me while she hooked me up to the machine and ran some tests, then with a big smile told me she'd go have the neurologist interpret the EEG results and have him come in to see me. The smile on her face was very comforting for me to see. I had a feeling I was going to be okay. Although I was a bit afraid to fall asleep, I couldn't help dozing while I waited for the neurologist.

About an hour later, the neurologist came in. He was very suave-looking, wearing what had to be a custom-made suit and expensive Italian shoes. He introduced himself as Dr. Maracle and said, "I might have to change my name to 'Miracle' instead now that I have a miracle patient. I had thought you might end up in a chronic vegetative state, but your EEG is normal, and I believe you're going to have a full recovery." He went on to perform some additional neurological tests and told me that he wanted to keep me in the hospital for one more day for observation, and then would discharge me to a local rehabilitation hospital for a week or so to do some intensive physical and occupational therapy and get my strength back. He said, "For every day you're in the hospital and bedridden, you lose 3% of your physical conditioning. Being comatose makes it worse because you're even less active than other patients; so it's important that you really work with the people at the rehab hospital to get back to your former strength. Once you're back to work, I'll want you on light duty for a bit, but before long you should be good as new."

Dr. Maracle could see that all the sudden activity and excitement were taking their toll, so he stood up and told me to get some rest and he'd be back to see me in the morning. As he was leaving, I sleepily asked, "Hey, Doc? You any relation to the Red Wings' former goalie, Norm Maracle? I always liked him." I still have no idea what he said, because I was asleep before I even heard his response.

Chapter 31

The next time I woke up, I started thinking that I need to stay awake this time. After losing a week and half of my life, I wanted to soak in as much activity and information as I could. I wondered whether all my friends and family had written me off as a goner. I hate to admit it, but I probably would if I came and visited somebody in a coma from which they might never wake up.

Next thing I knew, Gabby walked into my hospital room. In my scratchy, gravelly voice I said, "Well, you're a sight for sore eyes." Gabby's eyes lit up when she heard me speak, and she burst into tears. She covered her face with shaking hands, then looked upward and said, "Thank you, God." She said, "I can't believe my eyes; I've been coming here every other day praying to God that you would wake up."

"Thank God you didn't write me off," I said to Gabby. "I figured everybody else must have by now. I have a lot of questions. I've been unconscious for 11 days and I'm sure a lot of things have changed, so I need you to fill me in and get me up to speed with what's been going on."

She said, "I'll do my best, but my answers may not be satisfactory to you." "Can you please tell me if Maverick survived that gunfight?" I asked. "I need to know if he's okay. And what about Larry? The last time I saw him he appeared to have a neck injury and he had a big ugly horse convulsing on his legs."

Just as Gabby was starting to answer my questions, Dr. Schmidt walked in and said to Gabby,

"We need to talk before you talk to the patient." They went in the other room and spoke for a minute, and when Gabby came back she told me the doctor did not want her to give me too much information too quickly because it might cause me stress. I told Gabby, "You've known me for the better part of ten years. You know I can handle it. Please bring me up to speed. Not knowing is more stressful for me than anything."

Gabby agreed, and went on to say, "There was a hell of a gunfight at the 4th of July parade. I was on duty in a different part of the county and I'm glad I didn't see it. I've spoken to many other deputies that were there that day, and every time I hear about it, it's like having my guts ripped out."

"Let me start by telling you Maverick will make a full recovery. He was lucky that two of the three bullets just grazed him. The third bullet went into his leg but fortunately didn't hit any bones. He's still off work, but I believe he'll be going back on desk duty in a few days. You know how he hates paperwork and reports, so he'll probably be lobbying to get out on patrol as soon as possible. Larry is taking a month off and is expected to make a full recovery as well. The vertebrae in his neck were not broken, thank God, but he's undergoing physical therapy. By the way, both Maverick and Lieutenant Davison received commendations for bravery. Larry's horse received a funeral with honors."

"All we need to do now is get you some intensive therapy at the rehab hospital – Dr. Schmidt told me that's where you're headed – and get you back to work. It's hard to believe that all three of you are going to make a full recovery; any or all of you could have been killed."

"Have you talked to any members of my family?" I asked. Gabby said, "Yes, your mother has been up here every day, I believe. I've seen her a few times when I've come up to see you. And your kids have been here a lot. They're so worried about you." I asked, "Did everybody write me off?" Gabby said, "Not me, Patty. Never."

Gabby got a faraway look in her eye, and I couldn't help wondering what she was thinking. She shook her head and said, "I'm just overwhelmed. Walking in expecting to see you still comatose, and instead hearing you speak to me was just...I'm going to need to leave now and come back in a couple days. Will I hurt you if I give you a hug?" I smiled at her and said, "You'd hurt me if you didn't give me one." As we hugged, I inhaled the light, fresh scent of her hair and felt truly alive for the first time since I'd awakened from the coma.

I made up my mind right then and there that I was going to get out of this bed, make a full recovery and get back to work for the sake of my coworkers and my loved ones. The nurse came in and I told her my plan. She admonished me to slow down and take my time, but I said, "I don't have any more time to waste. I've been here for almost two weeks and I want to get better and get back to my life. I need to get things back to the way they were."

She said, "In that case, I'll get Dr. Schmidt to order a physical therapy assessment; it's possible we might even be able to get that going today, but tomorrow at the latest. What we need to do first is dangle you." "Excuse me?" I laughed. "Dangle me?" The nurse smiled and said, "That means we have you just sit on the edge of the bed and get your bearings. No standing up, just sitting on the edge of the bed with your legs over the edge. You've been lying down ever since you got here, so you'll likely be light-headed just sitting up." She chuckled and said, "Everyone in your family said you're stubborn as hell and strong as a mule. I see what they all meant."

My nurse managed to get the order for a PT assessment from Dr. Schmidt and even found a physical therapist who could do the assessment that same day. The dangling went well; I was just a bit light-headed for a minute or so, but the longer I sat on the edge of the bed, the more normal I felt. The physical therapist, with the help of an assistant, even let me stand up for a moment to get my bearings. She wouldn't let me walk yet, but she said she didn't think I'd need to stay in the rehab hospital more than a few days, then continue the PT on an outpatient basis. Dr. Schmidt stopped in to say that the physical therapist gave him a very encouraging report about my physical strength and mental determination. He said, "I'm going to discharge you to the rehab hospital tomorrow pending the results of some tests I want to run before you go. If all the tests look good, you're out of here in the morning. I have to tell you, this day did not go at all as I expected." He paused for a moment, then said, "It appears that something has happened to you that I don't completely understand. Your recovery is remarkable, and I may want to write this up as a case study for publication in a medical journal." I wasn't sure exactly what I was feeling – slightly scared, excited, intimidated, impatient – and I just kept telling the doctor the same thing repeatedly: "Get me the fuck on out of here."

The next morning, with all my tests looking great, I was discharged and transferred to the rehab hospital. I was a little embarrassed when Dr. Schmidt, Dr. Maracle and the entire nursing staff for that ward lined up and applauded as I was wheeled out in a wheelchair. There were a lot of teary-looking, happy faces, and although it was embarrassing, I was also proud that I was making such fast progress.

I got admitted to the rehab hospital and settled in, and they put me right to work with the first PT session of the day. Every day I would have morning and afternoon sessions of physical therapy and occupational therapy, and the medical director made a point of letting me know that this wasn't going to be like what he termed "pansy-ass outpatient PT". I told him, "Good! I want them to work me to the very outer limits of my abilities, so I can get home and go back to work ASAP."

As it turned out, I was only in the rehab hospital for five days. The therapists, nurses and medical director were amazed at the progress I was making once they learned the story of how I'd ended up there. While I was there, I had a full complement of people who came to visit me regularly. All my family. The chief, Maverick, the lieutenant, Gabby. Even Larry stopped by one day when he was out on patrol. We briefly talked about what happened on the 4th of July and everybody said they just wanted to move on. I was starting to feel like I was engaged with life again and that I truly had a future.

After undergoing one last round of tests, PT and OT assessments, EKG, echocardiogram, x-rays, blood work and a complete physical, the medical director gave me a clean bill of health and told me I was cleared to return to full duty as tolerated. He warned me I might find it necessary to work light duty at first if being on patrol was too tiring, but that he was leaving that up to my discretion depending on how I felt. I contacted the chief, who said, "I'm going to have you work with Peter for a while to get readjusted."

Chapter 32

The chief called me into his office. He wanted to tell me that he was having trouble covering security at the high school football games. The chief also mentioned that when he needed me to work with Peter, he wanted me to keep an eye on him because he'd been having trouble at the school. The chief also wanted me to submit a report to him after the assignment any time I worked with Peter.

> *Peter Latoya. In his early forties, Peter was a somewhat sloppy guy who had the assignment of school liaison officer. The way Peter told the story, he started out life in the Army, went to college on the G.I. Bill to study criminal justice, and after graduating from the police academy he got a job with a nearby police department. He worked there for about two years before joining the village police department.*

When I was first introduced to Peter I liked him, but my instincts told me there was something peculiar about him that I couldn't put my finger on. When he first came to the department he worked afternoons as road patrol. I know the field training officer, Maverick, spent additional time with him and retrained him on several occasions. After many assignments the chief and lieutenant decided to place him as a school liaison officer.

That evening, I reported to the squad room at 6:00 and had a quick chat with Peter. We came up with a game plan. I would work the inside of the football stadium and he would work the parking lot outside. At halftime we could switch places. Everything was routine. The buzzer went off at halftime. I tried to call Peter on the radio, but he wouldn't answer. I left the stadium and walked out into the parking lot. When I got to the cruiser, I saw that Peter was behind the wheel with his head back against the headrest and appeared to be sound asleep. It occurred to me that this would be a great opportunity to take a few pictures with my cell phone. After all, the chief had asked for a report and as the saying goes, a picture is worth a thousand words. After taking photos from many angles I put my cell phone away and knocked on the window. I crouched down on my hands and knees next to the door of the cruiser pounding on the window and then popped right up into his face.

As he awoke with a start, Peter was not happy. He rolled down the window, and I told him, "If you're getting paid you should be awake. I called you on the radio a few times, but you never answered."

He started to tell me about his family situation, all the troubles he was having at home and how he wasn't getting much sleep. I listened patiently, shook my head and said, "It sounds like you need to make some tough decisions."

We switched assignments as planned. He wanted to go into the stadium and I worked the parking lot. Somewhere around 9:00 Peter called me on the radio and told me there was a fight in the stadium. I came in to assist him. We broke up the fight and returned the teenagers to their parents and told them it was time for them to leave the game.

After the game Peter wanted to return to the station. I told him, "We better stick around till everybody leaves the school property because you never know what's going to happen after a game."

Around 9:45 we got a call that there was a large fight on Bartholomew Street. I jumped in the cruiser with Peter and said, "Let's go; hit it." He paused for a few moments and said, "Probably not a big fight. Let's just go back to the station." I told him, "We have an obligation to check it out and take a report." He stalled me for about two more minutes before I ordered him out of the driver's seat, told him to jump in the passenger seat and we were going to the fight on Bartholomew Street. He reluctantly agreed, and we took off to the call. By the time we arrived, the fight had broken up and there were a few kids in the street with some parents. All the parents demanded to know what had taken us so long; they had been waiting ten minutes

I thought to myself, "This report the chief wants on Peter is getting longer and uglier by the minute."

Chapter 33

It was a Wednesday afternoon in August 2005. The 31st, to be exact. One of those dates you don't forget. I was down in the training room at the sheriff's department with the whole crew. I was sitting next to Maverick and he was espousing his usual perfectionist mantra and gripes. I started in on my customary speech, that we live in a very imperfect world and we need to find a little acceptance. I said, "Study a little bit of philosophy and you will figure out there is some imperfection woven into the human condition."

We were finishing a continuing education class on the use of spike stripes when the county's emergency manager came in and announced that FEMA was looking for volunteers to help in New Orleans after Hurricane Katrina. He asked that anyone interested please see him after the meeting. I immediately said, "Hey, Mav, let's go." Maverick shot back, "Patty, are you fucking nuts? That's a disaster zone. It'll be total chaos. I wouldn't go there no matter how much they paid me."

Maverick said, "Mark my words, if you go down there you'll come back either scarred, injured, ill or fucking dead." I was disappointed by his statement, but I knew I was going to investigate it and find out more about the relief effort after Hurricane Katrina. After the training I met with the emergency manager, who said, "Here is the website. Call me if you have any questions."

I visited about a dozen websites and talked to five or six different administrators from FEMA who explained to me what they were looking for in volunteers. The federal government would compensate me. I would need to get a leave of absence approved by my chief for around six weeks before they could explain anything further.

I ran the idea by the chief, who said, "That's a long shot and it sounds very dangerous. Do you know the odds of making it out of there unscathed?" I said explained to him that I knew what I was considering doing was dangerous, but I still needed to make a decision of conscience and follow through. The chief said, "I'm very proud of you even though I think this is a questionable decision."

The chief went on to say, "I'm thinking about taking a leave of absence also, to go to work for the State Department. I would be working for the Army as a teacher over in Afghanistan. I'm planning on taking a year-long leave of absence to go visit my old friends in the Army."

Over the course of numerous discussions with the FEMA administrator I explained that I had Police, Fire and EMS experience. In addition, I was a certified scuba diver or underwater navigation specialist. The FEMA administrator said, "Those are great skills, but right now we need someone in transportation, ground search and rescue, and processing of deceased persons." I explained to the FEMA administrator that I'd be willing to fill in any position he had, to do my part in the relief effort.

I told the FEMA administrator that ideally, the type of assignment I was looking for would be if they could attach me to a Coast Guard rescue helicopter. I enjoy being on the wire, lowered down to rooftops to rescue people from the flood water. I explained to him that swift water rescue by air would be the ideal assignment for me considering all my training – Police, Fire, EMS and Sheriff's Department Dive Team. The FEMA administrator paused for a moment and said, "Yes, you do possess all the proper training for that assignment, but I don't know if I can place you there. You may have to be on the ground getting your feet wet, searching abandoned structures looking for survivors, and handling retrieval and processing of deceased persons. I paused for a moment and said, "If that's all you got for me, I'll take it." Then I involuntarily swallowed hard.

The FEMA administrator said, "It'll take seven days for me to process this. Pack your bags and get your legal affairs in order, talk to your wife and kids and let them know you'll be gone for six weeks and that you may or may not be able to contact them often because you'll be working under some of the most difficult circumstances of your entire life. Many people who return from this assignment come back injured or ill, so plan accordingly. You will be receiving a letter from the President of the United States thanking you for your service during this emergency. We will compensate you for any lost wages from your police department salary during your leave of absence, and we will also compensate your police department for any overtime they pay to cover for your absence."

I was puzzled by other people's trepidation. Maybe I was making a poor decision, maybe I was taking too big a chance at this stage in my life and career. I called Maverick and told him that I was heading down to New Orleans. He paused and swallowed audibly, and said, "I respect your decision even though I think you're a little crazy. By the way, make sure your will is filled out and leave me all your life insurance."

On my flight down to New Orleans, I put my feet up and tried to get comfortable. I thought maybe this could be the biggest adventure of my life. Then I thought it was more likely to just be six weeks in hell. I tried to fall asleep, but Arlo Guthrie was keeping me awake; I had his song "The City of New Orleans" on a continuous loop in my head. Yeah, I knew I was on a plane, not a train called The City of New Orleans, but it was stuck in my head anyway. "Nighttime on The City of New Orleans…"

Chapter 34

When I got to the emergency station, I met my liaison officer from FEMA, who advised me that I would be attached to a National Guard unit out of Shreveport, Louisiana with other police officers and firefighters from across the country attached to this National Guard division. The primary responsibilities would be search and rescue. He provided me with training, equipment and emergency contact information, then introduced me to my commanding officer. I was pleasantly surprised to learn that my commanding officer was also a police officer on leave from a police department in Massachusetts.

We struck up a conversation. He explained to me that we had a very difficult mission; the rescue effort was running 24/7. I was assigned to a squad that would be working 12 hours a day, seven days a week, 7 p.m. to 7 a.m. I asked, "84 hours a week, is that correct?" He said that until circumstances changed, we would be required to work 84 hours a week for the next six weeks.

He went on to say, "You will be provided with a limited amount of water, military rations, uniforms and equipment. I suggest that you manage these resources sparingly. Most of the water down here is contaminated, so you will be provided with bottled water. It may or may not be enough for your mission. I strongly suggest you don't drink any of the tap water."

He continued, "Other rescue workers that we have here are currently in the hospital suffering from an ugly intestinal infection caused by the contaminants in the water. Be advised that the water is very dangerous, and we don't even know all the contaminants in the water. Don't drink any of it; it could be a matter of life or death."

The commanding officer walked me into a briefing room where he had a map of the lower 9th Ward. It was broken down into zip codes with landmarks such as post offices, police stations, fire stations and other government buildings.

He explained to me that when we went out on patrol at 7 p.m., our primary responsibility would be search and rescue of at least two specific zip codes. We would also be in charge of security at all city, county and federal buildings. Securing property and materials at government buildings would be a priority.

After eating a light meal and getting some refreshments, the day shift search and rescue company came in and gave us a short briefing of what they had accomplished today and made a suggestion on what we might try to accomplish on our 12-hour night shift. They advised us that there were many looters, many people with firearms, and many people setting fire to buildings and vehicles, probably for insurance fraud.

We went out on a patrol in missions and made quite an impact. The number of people rescued and with medical emergencies was overwhelming. Transporting people from the lowlands to the higher grounds was our major responsibility. I lost count of how many hundreds of people we moved to safety.

At the Superdome, which was elevated about 30 feet above the water, we were starting to make substantial progress on the relief effort. The Superdome had not been damaged by the storm. This was the ideal location to set up the FEMA Emergency Management station. Most FEMA directives came from this office.

After about 4½ weeks I woke up with a pounding headache and intestinal cramps. I thought back to the previous day's mission. I had run out of water halfway through my assignment and got so dehydrated that I was dizzy. In a panic, I drank a little bit of the tap water in a dilapidated building. Around 5:00 that afternoon my commanding officer suggested that I go be checked out by the medical control division. The doctor concluded that I was suffering from a critical intestinal infection and needed to be taken by airvac to a hospital outside of the disaster zone.

Shortly before the medics loaded me into the helicopter, the pain became so intense that I lost consciousness. When I woke up, I was in an Army hospital somewhere in northern Florida. Nobody really wanted to explain too many things to me except that I was critically ill. I was having disturbing memories of when I was in the hospital after the shootout at the 4th of July parade. Nobody would tell me anything then, either. The FEMA administrator called me on the phone to tell me that my mission was over. I needed to be transported back home to Michigan so family members could continue my medical care. After about three weeks at home I was healed and ready to return to work.

Chapter 35

It was a quiet Saturday afternoon and Maverick and I were off to a very routine day. The only issue we had was a train coming through town. The train broke down on the tracks and we had to set up a detour to get cars down Main Street. The Canadian National Railway mechanics came out, repaired the engine and got the train off the tracks through town. About an hour later, Maverick and I were back at the police station. When he went to unfasten his seatbelt, it caught the front of the Taser cartridge, which broke. Maverick said, "Holy shit…looks like I've broken the Taser. I wonder if there's an extra one in the equipment room." We went to the equipment room to look for a second Taser but couldn't find one. Maverick said, "Well, keep in mind that my Taser's out of service, so if we get in a throwdown today you're going to need to move to pepper spray."

While out on patrol, I didn't think much about it. Using the Taser isn't a daily occurrence, so it didn't seem like that big a deal. A couple hours later we got called to a domestic disturbance. The person making the phone call was sitting in a car on Carlsbad Avenue. We pulled up behind the car and got out to find a middle-aged woman and her daughter, both visibly shaken. The woman explained that she had argued with her husband and that he kicked them out of the house. As we were getting the details, a small silver car came racing up the street behind us and slammed on the brakes.

I commented to Maverick, "I think the husband has arrived. Let the games begin." The husband started to scream at the wife, who told us, "That's my husband.

You guys better arrest him." Maverick and I had had a few encounters with this guy in the past. He was bad news. His name was Fred, but everybody in town just called him 'Crunch'. He was a big guy, approximately 275 pounds and 6'5", and a semi-professional bodybuilder. He had an intimidating presence. He'd probably lifted weights for 15 or 20 years while taking buckets of steroids. He almost looked a bit like a human monster. The whites of his eyes had a waxy yellow appearance consistent with chronic steroid overdose. This was the second time I had seen Crunch in a full-blown case of 'roid rage', possibly also stoked by methamphetamines.

When he approached, he looked to be possibly in a drug-induced manic rage. His forehead and neck veins were protruding, and he was screaming so loud and fast that it was hard to even understand him. I saw him run at Maverick, so I maneuvered to take him at the flank. He stopped about 15 feet from Maverick and started screaming, "I'm going to kill both of you fucking cops. That bitch wife of mine is always kicking me out of house and fucking me over. I'm fucking sick of this shit and I'm ready to die today, so do whatever you gotta do."

As Maverick pulled the Taser out of his duty belt, the cartridge fell to the ground and he shot me a quick look that was like 'what do we do now?'. Crunch was facing Maverick head-on. I was at Maverick's 4 o'clock position trying to decide if I was going to pepper spray Crunch. There was a lot of cross-shouting between Crunch, his wife and Maverick. I could see the situation was escalating quickly. I made a quick tactical calculation. Maverick was holding a taser that was out of service, and pepper spray was never going to stop Crunch. I flashed back to a discussion that I'd had with Lieutenant Dan about two months earlier. He'd told me, "If you ever have a fight with Crunch you probably won't survive. He's a cold-blooded killer who's been in and out of prison his whole adult life."

I glanced at Maverick, who looked terrified. I'd never seen him appear to be afraid of anything before. The expression on his face made me decide to put the pepper spray away and get my gun out. I pulled my gun out of my duty belt. I yelled at Crunch to freeze. He turned toward me and saw the barrel of my gun pointing at his face and started to scream at me, "You cops don't have the balls to pull that trigger. Don't waste my time."

Crunch's wife cried out, "Don't shoot my husband! I still love him." Things calmed for a moment as Crunch looked over at his wife. I said to him calmly, "Look, Fred, we've dealt with you in the past, and I know you're not a bad guy. At this point, right now all we have a domestic disturbance – no big deal – but if you charge at me, my partner is going to be forced to shoot you because we can't overpower you. You decide your fate."

Within about five seconds the demons that seemed to be possessing Fred left his body and he started to think more clearly. He started to shake his head and said, "I almost died. This is such bullshit, all this over a stupid argument with my wife." He put his hands up and said, "I surrender."

Maverick handcuffed Fred and put him in the back of the cruiser, then went up to his wife and said, "We're going to have to arrest and hold your husband for 24 hours, charge him with domestic violence and let him cool down. After 24 hours you can come down and bond him out if you want, or file for divorce, or take whatever action you and your lawyer decide is in your best interest."

After we got Fred booked in the county jail and were driving back to the police station, Maverick said, "Looks like you were right to move toward fatal force. Considering that my Taser was out of service and pepper spray never would have worked on that guy, that's the appropriate amount of force to be used in the situation."

"Did you notice the t-shirt Freddy was wearing?" Maverick asked me. I said, "I wasn't paying any attention to Freddy's shirt because I was focused on saving your ass. Why?" Chuckling, Maverick said, "His t-shirt said 'Jesus saves'. Just think, if you'd shot Freddy, you'd have been known as the cop who had to shoot the man wearing the 'Jesus saves' shirt." We were both laughing so hard that Maverick had to pull over so we could compose ourselves.

Chapter 36

After working a large volume of cases as a police officer, you start to see a pattern. This pattern becomes very familiar after you work several cases in a small town. After taking a complaint you usually make contact with two different people. Each has a different perspective on the complaint. Both parties believe that by exaggerating certain details, they can make themselves look good and make the other party appear to be the guilty one.

It's comical to see the ridiculous lengths to which some people will go thinking they can pull the wool over your eyes. What's notable is that most people are very emotional when they contact the police and they don't realize that their logic is not strung together very well.

One Sunday evening I was contacted by a mother regarding a child custody and visitation issue. I took a few notes as the mother told me that she had dropped the child off at the father's house on Friday. The child was supposed to be returned to her house by 6:00 Sunday evening. I tried to interrupt to ask her if the father was ever late bringing the child back before, but she refused to answer my questions. She started in on a lengthy rant, explaining that her ex-husband was a 'piece of shit loser' who had no life. She went on at length, saying that her ex-husband was angry, violent, dangerous and manipulative, and that she'd escaped the marriage through a very ugly and painful divorce.

My first thought was that I was going to have to go remove the child from the father's house, and he was probably going to be a hardened felon with weapons and a violent past. I thought about getting on the radio to get backup. A wise instinct, though, told me that this woman may be playing some theatrics. By her loud and agitated description of her ex-husband, you'd think I'd have to call the SWAT team to remove the child from a barricaded firearms situation. Something told me, however, that this may not be the case.

I said, "Before we go any further I'm going to need your ex-husband's name. I might need to run him through our database to see what his prior convictions are." The woman glared at me; she really wasn't ready for this question and didn't want to answer it. She wanted to continue to talk about her ex-husband's flaws and violent behavior.

I looked her in the eye and spoke up in a stern voice, "If you want to get your child back you're going to need to tell me your ex-husband's name. We can't proceed with this complaint until you give me all the details." Her face betrayed her emotions; she was angry and frustrated. She started to shake her finger at me, but when she saw me raise one eyebrow on my stern face she said, "Well, let's just try to get my child back."

She gave me her husband's name and it sounded familiar. I said with a straight face, "How funny! Do you realize that your ex-husband shares the same name as the principal at the high school? Odd. And what is his current address, ma'am? Her face was flushed with embarrassment. She started to stutter, "What...what....what principal at the high school…" and she mumbled the address. I said, "How funny is that? I'm pretty sure the principal lives on that same street."

She said, "This is not going the way I expected. I was hoping you could just pick up my son and bring him home. I don't really want to talk about anything else. I said, "Just one more question. I need your ex-husband's date of birth to make sure I have the right guy."

I told her to sit tight at her house and I should have her son back to her in a few hours. "I need to run up to the station and check the records. I'll give you a call when I have your son in the cruiser and I'm heading back to your house. She shook her head and began to wring her hands, looking very embarrassed. She said, "I really have nothing else to say to you. Just please get my son back home."

I ran over to the station and ran a criminal history on both the ex-husband and her. After triple-checking all the records, I confirmed my earlier suspicion that her ex-husband was, in fact, the principal at the high school. I believed she was trying to exaggerate the situation in pursuit of bringing charges against the ex-husband. Interestingly, a check of her criminal history revealed that she had several felony convictions and was currently on probation for drug offenses. His history, unsurprisingly, was pristine. She was good at selling images of people that are not so flattering. I was seeing the truth in the complaint and was disappointed by her lies and irritated by her wasting my time.

I drove over to the home of the child's father, who was, in fact, the principal of the high school. He stated that his ex-wife had said that she would be out of town until 8:00 Sunday night and had asked him to keep their son until she returned. I advised him that she was not being truthful. He said that five years previously, his wife had developed a drug habit and he discovered she'd been selling off marital assets to feed her drug problems.

He went on to say that his former mother-in-law had staged an intervention and the result was a divorce. We were finishing up, so I looked at my watch; it was 7:45. I told the father to run the child over to his ex-wife's house and that I would follow.

When we got to her home, I asked her to step outside with her ex-husband and me. The three of us had a brief chat and I explained to her, "You're on probation and yet for some reason you thought it was a good idea to set up your ex-husband and file a false police report. Sounds like a good way to end up back in jail and lose custody of your son permanently." She shook her head, cleared her throat and said, voice shaking, "I'm done here." With that, she grabbed the child, walked through the door and slammed it behind her.

I gave the ex-husband my card and told him that I would be writing up a detailed report of this incident and asked him to call me if he had any further problems like this one. He thanked me profusely for investigating so thoroughly before taking any action. He struck me as a responsible, loving parent who just wanted to put the past behind him and find a way to amicably and successfully co-parent the child he unfortunately shared with a vindictive, manipulative felon of an ex-wife.

Chapter 37

It was a wintry Friday night around 11:30 and the boys and I were upstairs at the firehouse playing a game of pool when the tones went off. Dispatch said that there was a report of a car through the ice near the south boat launch at Hoover Lake. We suited up in turnout gear, grabbed the boat and called dispatch stating, "En route to Hoover Lake near the south boat launch."

When we arrived on scene it was dark. All we could see was the rear deck lid of a late model Oldsmobile sticking out of the water; the rest of the car was not visible. We began to get the equipment together – an ice water rescue boat, ladders and Stokes baskets. Willie and Glen were the first out on the ice, crawling across the ladders. They radioed back, telling me to slide an axe out onto the ice so they could break the back window out. Glen got back on the radio, "We have the car occupied by two teenaged boys." When Glen got to the first boy – the driver – he was blue and not breathing. We got the Stokes basket across the ice to him while Glen and Willie started a rapid extrication of both boys from the car. When we got the driver out we started CPR; shortly after that, we got the passenger out. He was hypothermic, convulsing and choking. We were pretty sure we could save one of their lives. As Glen and Willie were stabilizing the passenger, the driver regained consciousness and began choking and coughing up icy water.

The driver could barely speak, but kept mumbling, "My mom's going to kill me for wrecking her car." Just about the time we thought we had both boys saved, the driver went into cardiac arrest. We started CPR and were trying to reduce the hypothermia. After getting both boys in Stokes baskets and getting across the ladders and off the ice, we were getting the driver stabilized again and getting him into the ambulance when the second ambulance showed up. We gave a brief summary to the ambulance driver and handed off the driver for transport to the hospital.

The passenger was in and out of consciousness. He had gone into cardiac arrest but then regained a slow, weak heartbeat and began to gurgle and breathe. We began to think we could possibly save him. After getting the passenger stabilized and loading him into the second ambulance, we gave them a rundown on his condition. He started to breathe on his own and have a normal heartbeat, but we were concerned about the amount of time he'd been in cardiac arrest without oxygen perfusing his brain.

Now that both patients had been stabilized and transported, we began to stabilize the vehicle so we could remove it from the lake. Willie tied some lines and prepared the vehicle for removal from the ice. One of the local wrecker drivers showed up, and we explained to him that we would drag the cable across the ice and hook it up to the rear of the vehicle. He was in charge of winching the vehicle back up onto the shore.

After removing the vehicle, getting it towed and making some phone calls, we put up caution tape around the area with some signs reading, "DANGER – Stay Off Ice".

We returned to the station and put the vehicle and equipment back into service. Later, we received the good news that both boys would be fine. One was treated and released, and the other spent three days in the hospital. Although we're trained to keep our emotions compartmentalized, it's hard to do that when children are in danger. The two boys were incredibly lucky, but I think we all felt secretly proud that we'd saved their lives.

Chapter 38

It was the week of Halloween and I had been working first shift most of the week when, on Wednesday, the chief called me into his office and said, "I need you to work Halloween evening with Maverick. You'll be teaming up in a two-man car. I know there will be a number of complaints and I need both of you with your heads screwed on straight." I looked straight at the chief and said, without any hesitation, "Yes, sir."

On Halloween evening I walked into the squad room and met up with Maverick. He was in a bubbly mood; he kept spouting one of his 'Maverickisms' – "show up wearing a bell and tell 'em to go to hell". I knew we were off to an eventful shift. I walked out to the cruiser and gave it a full inspection, checking the oil, tires, radio, computer, shotgun, machine gun, even the gas mask.

My energy level was low because I'd gone from working day shift to night shift, but within about ten minutes of being in the car with Maverick, my energy level rushed up to 100%. I had a feeling that we were going to do some important work that evening; I just didn't know what it would be.

Maverick being the comedian that he was, said, "Let's start our shift off by driving through the cemetery. After all, it's Halloween. I want to make sure all the people in the cemetery belong there." He added, "Last year, two teenaged boys dressed up like zombies and were stumbling around in front of the cemetery by the road."

After we completed our patrol through the cemetery, an all-points bulletin came across the radio. "Be on the lookout for a silver Ford pickup truck, a drive-off from the gas station, heading west on G Avenue." The only other description was that there was a large decal of a horse on the back window.

I said to Maverick, "Sounds like that Ford pickup truck is coming our way." When he didn't respond, I looked over at him and he had a puzzled look on his face. I could see the many gears spinning inside his head. He was slightly preoccupied, in a highly analytical moment. What came out of his mouth next blew my mind. He said, "I bet that joker drove off with gas at the Speedway station and maybe the truck belongs to Johnson's Horse Farm here in town. I'll bet you a nickel he drives by."

I replied, "I don't think we could be that lucky." We struck up a conversation about the local Halloween activities around the community. A few minutes later I glanced to the right and saw a pickup truck go by; on the back window was a huge decal that said, "Johnson's Horse Farm".

I said, "Hey, Mav…I think that's the drive-off from the Speedway." When we pulled out into the roadway and activated the lights, I could see that it was a silver Ford pickup truck with a big horse decal in the back window and two young guys riding in it.

When we made the traffic stop, the driver of the vehicle asked why we'd pulled him over. Maverick asked, "Did you drive off without paying for gas from the Speedway gas station over in Prairie Township?

The driver said, "I pumped my gas, then walked into the Speedway, told them what pump number I was at and asked for some smokes. The attendant said your total is $5.49, and I totally forgot about the $42.00 in fuel."

Maverick gave the driver a really stern look and said, "If you turn around and drive back to Speedway, I'll follow you there and you'll pay them the $42.00 for the gas. That way I won't have to arrest you for larceny from a gas station.

The driver said, "That sounds like an offer I can't refuse." We followed him back and made contact with the gas station attendant. I asked, "Is this the truck that drove off earlier?" He said that it was. I said, "Would you like to press charges?" He said, "No, as long as I get the money and my cash drawer is not short." The driver hastily paid for the gas, and I told him, "Now that you have paid for your fuel you're free to go." As I was leaving, I turned back to the attendant and said, "By the way, the horse decal was the clue we needed to catch the drive-off." He smiled and said, "Glad that worked." He thanked us for our help, and we went on our way.

Maverick and I went back to the station, where he flipped a quarter and said, "Heads you write the report, tails I write it." The quarter bounced twice and landed on the desk, heads up. I settled in to write the report.

Chapter 39

It was a beautiful day out on the lake when I woke up. I looked out from the deck and saw the sun rising on the lake and decided to pick up some fuel for the pontoon boat. I would probably cruise it all afternoon. Shortly before heading to the gas station, some friends called and invited themselves over by announcing, "We'll be at your dock by noon. Be ready for a long day on the lake." With a big smile, I said I'd be ready to go by noon. I would have enjoyed a solitary day of cruising the lake alone with my thoughts, but I was more in the mood for the company of good friends. I figured since I was going out for fuel, I'd better pick up some beverages, ice, and something to throw on the grill later.

We spent most of the day on the lake boating and laughing. Later that night, tired from the sun and the company, I was in bed by 10:00. In the early morning hours, somewhere around 4:00, the alert tone went off on my pager. It was dispatch saying, "We have a report of smoke and flames coming from the house across from 213 Main Street." I jumped out of bed thinking, "Duty calls".

When I got into my truck to respond to the call there was traffic on the radio. Rob, a fellow volunteer firefighter who lived down the street from the address involved, was on scene giving a size-up on the fire. He said, "Two stories, single-family dwelling, wood construction, fully involved fire. Please respond with all equipment and personnel." I was sure my best option was to swing by the firehouse and drive Engine 1512 unless I heard someone else pulling the engine on the radio before I got there.

As I pulled up to the station two other guys had beaten me there. "No time to talk," they yelled. "Get 1512 and we'll follow you in the rescue truck." As I pulled out, I thought the nearest fire hydrant would be at Davis and 6th Street. Better make the hydrant and lay hose up to the house.

> *Michael 'Mick' K. Donaldson, Firefighter/Paramedic. A complicated guy, Mick was part redneck with an Australian accent. His father was Australian, and his mother was a Georgia southern belle. On occasion, Mick's right eye twitched. He was very self-conscious about the twitch, which only made the eye twitch more.*

As I pulled up to the fire hydrant, Mick jumped out of the rescue truck and prepared the hydrant. Mick wrapped the five-inch hose around the base of the hydrant, stood on the hose and shouted, "Hit it!"

I looked out the side mirror from the driver seat and made eye contact with Mick. He gave me the nod and I laid the hose up to the house. The scene was abuzz with action, with two dozen firefighters on scene battling the blaze.

I checked in with the chief by radio. He said that I would be running the pumper. I was disappointed; I'd hoped Mick would get the pumper assignment, so I could do some aggressive interior firefighting. Search and rescue was my specialty.

I hit Mick up on the radio, but he was already suited up to go interior, so I guessed I would stay on the pumper for this fire. I had no idea what was inside the house, but later I was glad I was outside.

Later, after the fire was declared under control, the fire chief announced that the fire ground was declared a crime scene and to follow all procedures and protocols associated with this requirement. I knew instinctively that either someone died in the fire, or that the origin was arson. Later, after Mick came out of the fire, he spoke with me. He was troubled and was saying the same thing repeatedly. He said, "There's a dead young boy in there and the parents were making meth."

I tried to shake Mick out of his shock, but it was no use. He was in the grip of PTSD, post-traumatic stress disorder. Having been there before myself, I knew he would need counseling in a few days and although I was sad for him, I was relieved that it was him in that state, and not me. I felt his pain but knew it was his personal journey through hell. I had been there before and knew he would wash out in a week or two.

The coroner's truck arrived on scene, and I knew it was going to be a long night. As I shut down the pumper and started the post-fire cleanup, I thought about meth fires and the messes they make in people's lives. Drugs are powerful and dangerous things; that had been clearly demonstrated at this fire.

Chapter 40

It was 8:00 one morning when, after completion of the daily radio test, dispatch announced a work detail at the fire station. "We will be fire hose testing today. Please report to complete assignment." I thought I would swing by to help. Rolling hoses and cleaning after the test was a lot of work.

After laying out thousands of feet of hose and plugging the ends with a pressure gauge, all the hoses passed the test. We pulled new hose off the rack and replaced the hose on the fire truck, then washed and hung up the tested hose in the hose tower to dry.

The captain said, "Thanks, guys. Now let's eat lunch." After lunch we went back out to give the truck a final check. Just then alert tones went off at the station. Dispatch said, "Possible drowning in the pool at 314 Parkhurst Drive." We suited up and climbed onto the big red truck. We were a four-man crew – The captain, the lieutenant, John and me.

When we arrived on the scene, we found no one home. The captain said, "Go around to the back yard and check." I ran around the house and there was no pool, but I noticed a big fence next door. The captain said, "Let's check over the fence."

When we looked over the fence we saw an elderly man in a wheelchair, frantic and hyperventilating, and a baby face down in the pool. The captain shouted, "Over the fence! Get that baby out of the water!" John Kuiper was first over the fence.

John B. Kuiper. Sometimes called 'Hyper Kuiper', John had the true heart of a firefighter. He was a second-generation firefighter with the local fire department. He had started at the fire academy a couple of years before his father retired from the same fire department. He was the most dedicated and driven firefighter I've ever met. I felt honored to work with him. We had been in large structure fires together a couple of times. I had full confidence in his ability to rescue me if I got trapped.

John jumped right into the water, scooped up the baby and cleared the airway. I was standing next to the pool when John handed me the baby boy, and I was horrified when I saw that little face that was as blue as the little blue romper he was wearing. This was the first time I had ever seen a baby in full cardiac and respiratory arrest. I didn't have time to think; my training kicked in, and just as I started treatment the captain pushed me aside. He said, "Grab the First In bag and get me a one-way mask and the oxygen bottle." I was a bit relieved that he took the initiative to start patient care and put me into a secondary position. After he got the airway clear and started to pump the oxygen, the baby began to cough and scream. We rolled the baby over on his side to let his lungs clear. When the blue started to fade out of the baby's face and the pink color came back, I felt a tremendous sense of achievement. I was so caught up in the moment that everything around me faded out. I had tunnel vision and my only concern had been to get the infant breathing again.

The grandfather in the wheelchair pulled up behind me and said, emotionally, "Thank you." He had been there all along, but I never noticed him because I was too caught up in patient care. He told me that he had been babysitting the child and had accidentally left the door to the pool open. He was certain that his daughter and son-in-law would be down to the firehouse to thank us later that evening.

The captain had a few questions for the grandfather. He said to him, "When you dialed 911, the address was to the house next door. Do you have any idea why?" The grandfather said, "I live next door and I was calling you on my cordless phone." That's what had caused the confusion with dispatch. The ambulance showed up and we put the baby on the gurney and loaded it into the ambulance. The grandfather said again, with tears in his eyes, "I can't thank you enough!"

The captain turned to look at me while I was handing the baby off to the paramedics driving the ambulance. He said, "Since the grandfather is not able to ride with the baby to the hospital, it'll be your responsibility to accompany the baby with the ambulance crew down to the emergency room and turn the baby over to the ER doctor." When I arrived at the hospital with the paramedics, I briefed the doctor, quickly stating that we'd found the child face-down in the water and not breathing.

Later that evening, the baby's mother and father stopped by the firehouse on the way home to show us their beautiful, healthy baby boy and to thank us for getting him out of the water and breathing again.

The mother told us, "The doctors have checked him over and said he's fine, but they said that if he had been in the pool for another five minutes the outcome would've been totally different." The baby's parents were overcome with gratitude that beamed out of their hearts and eyes. This was the first time I had ever experienced such gratitude and appreciation, and it fueled my soul.

Chapter 41

My cell phone rang; I looked down and saw that it was Glen. He said, "Hey mister! You know what today is?" I replied, "No, is it your birthday? I hope not, because I didn't get you anything." "No, it's way better than that," said Glen. "It's Swift Water Training today at Station 15 at 7:00 p.m." Don't forget your towel because you might get wet." Then he laughed into the phone and said, "The chief said this training is mandatory. Will you be there?" I replied, "Well, yeah, if it's mandatory, it's mandatory." Glen said, "Great!" and promptly hung up.

I was entertained and a little concerned at the same time. I thought that Glen must be up to something because he rarely called me about training at the fire department. All day I found myself wondering, "What the hell is Glen up to?" Later, I was home eating dinner and looked up at the clock. It was 6:45, so I figured I'd better get up to the firehouse for training.

When I walked into the firehouse the training room was packed. It appeared that the chief's message had been received by everyone. All firefighters were present for training. The chief walked up to the podium and said, "Glad you all could make it to training tonight." He went on to say, "It's been six months since our last Swift Water Rescue Training. Considering that we have the Sawyer River running through the center of our town, it's amazing we haven't had a rescue call to the river this year."

The chief continued, "This training will be run by Glen, so I'll turn it over to him now." The chief sat down, and Glen took his place at the podium with a shit-eating grin on his face. Glen said, "The chief so graciously put me in charge of this training. As most of you know, I am an expert at swift water rescue. Your drill today will involve evolutions with the rope bag. Also, all of you will be required to make an evolution as the water rescue victim, so I hope you all like getting wet."

Glen turned to the chalkboard and drew a diagram of the river and shoreline. Then he explained the procedure for each evolution of training, and we split into teams. After the classroom portion of training, we all walked into the apparatus bay to get our equipment assignments.

I was assigned to Team 4, which consisted of the chief, John, Mick and me. We would be the fourth team to go. I thought, "This is perfect. We can watch the first three teams struggle with training and learn from their mistakes." Knowing Glen to be a taskmaster, I was prepared to get wet before our turn was up.

As our crew pulled Engine 1515 and headed to the boat landing on the east side of the river, Glen and Team 2 were set up across the river on the west side. The plan was to set up safe rope and anchor points upstream on both sides of the river. Teams 1 and 3 would be in their boats, stationary, 300 yards upriver. Downstream about 500 yards was a safety net across the whole river to catch anyone who missed the rope bag.

For the drill, the water victim would jump off the boat upstream. As they floated by, Teams 2 and 4 would take turns throwing a rope bag into the water for the victim so those of us on the shore could pull them in. Glen got on the radio and ordered Scott, the water victim on the upstream boat, to jump into the water. I knew he would be floating by in 45 seconds.

Chief was on deck with the rope bag and was shouting to Scott, telling him, "Get your hands up so I can throw the rope bag to you." As Scott floated by, the chief wound up and made a perfect throw to Scott, hitting him right in his hands. Scott got a grip on the rope and the chief pulled him to shore. Chief helped Scott out of the water, then turned to our crew and said, "That's how it's done."

After running the drill a few times, everyone was getting good at throwing the rope bag. Eventually, Glen got on the radio and announced that it was time for the teams to shift stations. Team 4 was dispatched to the boat upstream, and I knew it would soon be my turn in the water.

The chief volunteered to go first into the water, then said that I would be going in after he finished. Chief floated downriver and was pulled to shore. Moments later, Glen got on the radio and said, "Next victim." I checked my life vest and safety equipment. On cue, I jumped in with total faith in my crew to get me to shore. The operation went just as planned. After meeting up with Glen on shore I asked him, "When is it your turn to go in the water?" He just looked at me incredulously and said, "You kidding? No fucking way."

We were finished with training at the boat landing, and everyone was cleaning and storing the equipment. I walked up just as Glen was talking with Carl; they were in a heated argument. Glen said, "I'm running the training and I decide who's going in the water." The chief jumped in between the two of them, calming their tempers. Suddenly, Glen grabbed Carl and threw him into the river. The chief barked an order at Glen to go in and get Carl. Glen said, "Watch this," and he picked up a rope, lassoed Carl and pulled him to shore. Poor Carl looked confused and taken aback.

Everyone walked down to help Carl. Glen just stood there, laughing, and we recognized that Glen threw Carl in and Carl was trying to be a good sport about it. Chief was upset, but everyone else was enjoying a good laugh. After stowing all the equipment, we were headed back to the firehouse to put on dry clothes. During the field trip debriefing, the chief said, "That was a dangerous stunt with Carl. We had already removed the safety equipment from the water." He growled at Glen, "Don't do that again."

As we were all sitting in the training room the alert tones went off. Dispatch said, "We have a report of a man stuck in a swamp behind the house at 16529 Millard Road."

The chief looked at Glen first and then at me, saying, "You two take pumper 1611 and head to the call. John and I will follow you in the rescue rig." As Glen and I jumped into pumper 1611, I said, "Glen, this is kind of odd. We had a swift water rescue today and right after finishing up we get a man stuck in a swamp. I think you jinxed us. I hope you're ready to get your ass wet this time 'cause it's gonna be your turn."

As we made it out to the 16000 block of Millard Road, I said to Glen, "I believe it's the third house on the right past the big oak tree. Seems like I've been here before; I think there's an old man and a dog who are usually out walking in the street near this house."

We parked the 1611 truck in the driveway and spoke with a distraught elderly woman who said that the family dog had gotten caught out in the swamp and when her husband went out to get the dog, he got stuck in the swamp too. We could hear the dog barking and the man shouting for help. He was about 250 yards behind the house. The swamp was very low and there were marshy areas before we got to the swamp.

A few minutes later, the chief and John showed up in the rescue rig. We all put our heads together for a minute and decided that we would throw some ladders down through the marshy cattail area to make our way to the sandbar. From there, we'd run a pair of 1½" capped hoses. Glen would climb out on the hoses with a harness and rope to get to the man and the dog and bring them to dry land and safety.

It took us about 10 minutes to prep and set up the equipment we'd need to rescue the man and his dog. Glen made his way most of the way, and I went part of the way into the swamp with him. I could hear him speaking to the man stuck in the swamp, telling him, "Don't move or struggle; I'm going to throw you some rope and I need you to get the rope securely around you and the dog and then wait for instructions." I shouted back to the guys on dry land, "We're going to drag them all up onto solid ground." Once I was back up on solid ground, Chief, John and I got the rescue rope tied around our waists. We all leaned back and waited for Glen to make the call. Once Glen had the rope secured to the man and the dog, we all started to walk backward slowly, pulling Glen, the elderly man and the dog out of the dark, loamy swamp and up onto solid ground. It wasn't easy for Glen and the elderly man; they both made a few cursing comments during the painful extrication from the swamp.

Once the man and his dog were safe, we all had a quick huddle in the backyard. We were happy to see that neither the dog nor the old man was injured; they were muddy, but they were damn glad to be out of the swamp. The dog rolled around on the lawn trying unsuccessfully to get the mud off, which gave us all a good laugh. Just moments later, the man's wife came out carrying a pot of coffee and freshly-baked muffins on a tray. She was overjoyed to see her husband and dog out of the swamp and wanted to show her appreciation by sharing some hot coffee and goodies with us.

We were all filthy, wet and muddy, but the wife told us not to worry about that. We made our way up to the porch in the back of the house, where there was some light. We all had some of the most delicious hot coffee and freshly-baked muffins we'd ever had and talked about how we hoped the dog would never again make its way back out into the swamp chasing a bird.

The chief pulled out his clipboard and made a quick report of the couple's names and address and confirmed that the man did not want to be transported to the hospital to be checked out. The elderly man signed a release form and we thanked his wife for the hot coffee and delicious muffins.

After returning to the station, cleaning up all the dirty equipment and hose-washing our turnout gear, we stood in the apparatus bay – the chief, Glen and I – laughing and saying that we hoped we didn't have to go into a swamp ever again. That was one big ugly mess, and an ordeal to clean up our equipment afterward, but the freshly-baked muffins and the satisfaction we got out of successfully extricating the elderly man and his dog from the swamp made up for it.

Chapter 42

It was a Thursday afternoon around 4:00 when the phone rang. It was Maverick, speaking fast and loudly. "You wouldn't believe what happened when I was getting my scuba equipment serviced today. The owner of the dive shop said he won a free trip to Mexico to dive at a resort. A two-person vacation – and his wife can't get off work! You know what that means? All you need to do is talk the chief into letting both of us off work for the same week. Maybe one of the sheriff's deputies can come down and cover the overtime. Call Deputy McCloud – he's always looking for overtime!"

He continued, "Call McCloud first, make sure he can do it, then call the chief and tell him you got McCloud to cover the overtime. Then get your scuba gear over to the dive shop and have them check everything."

I said, "I've never done any salt-water diving. You have." Maverick went on, talking over me, "You wouldn't believe how clear the water is and the fish you will see! Tropical fish are so colorful and exotic, not like the trout and other fish you see in freshwater diving." Maverick was like a little boy at Christmas about the vacation, and I was excited too. When would we ever have a chance like this again?

Moments later, I was on the phone with McCloud, who was happy about the prospect of overtime. Next, I called the chief, who said I could have the time off since we'd already figured out everything to cover the overtime. I called Maverick back and excitedly said, "We're going to Mexico! Book me on the vacation!"

He said, "Get down to see the owner of the dive shop and tell him I sent you."

It was a week later, Friday afternoon, when I started to pack for my Sunday morning flight to Mexico. It all seemed to fall together too quickly and neatly. Maverick called and said, "Meet me at the gym; we can get a workout and finish making our travel plans." After the workout and a conversation, I felt like everything was covered. On Sunday morning, Maverick's wife, Helen, would drop us off at the airport.

As the plane took off for Mexico, I marveled at how this whole vacation had come together in just a week. After landing in Mexico, Maverick and I made our way to the resort. Everything was even more beautiful than I had expected. We really were in paradise.

We met with the instructor and the divemaster from the scuba dive school. They went on and on about safety and medical conditions like decompression sickness, otherwise known as the bends. After 20 minutes of repetition, my mind zoned out and I lost track of his message. A few times I looked over at Maverick, who was fully engaged in the instructions, and thought, "I've been scuba diving for eight years. I know what I'm doing." After class the two of us went to the bar to have dinner and drinks. At dinner, Maverick brought up the fact that I had never been diving in salt water and had never been to the depths that we might reach. I assured him that I could handle it.

The next morning, as we loaded up our equipment on the diving boat, the instructor looked at my equipment and found a problem with the regulator. I was surprised, as I'd had everything checked by the dive shop before I left home. Maverick suggested that I rent some equipment from the dive shop at the resort. I agreed, and the boat had to wait for almost 45 minutes for me to return with the equipment before they could leave, which irked many of the other scuba divers. The only equipment available had been set up with Nitrox. I had never used this type of equipment before. Maverick said, "You'll be fine; quit being a crybaby."

As we made it out into the ocean I was struck by the beauty of it all. The water was crystal blue and the waves were three-foot breakers. The dive boat was tricked out with all the equipment I could have ever imagined. We stopped about 300 yards offshore, and the captain announced that we were at the coral reef. Maverick and I went over all the safety systems and underwater communication signals with hand gestures for backup.

Maverick and I had been diving partners many times in fresh water, and we were both accomplished scuba divers and current members of the sheriff's department's water rescue diving team. We had full confidence in each other's abilities. Just before we went into the water we confirmed all the dive schedules and the parameters, even the time window for the dive. Maverick reminded me that this was my first time diving on Nitrox and there would be an adjustment period.

After about 15 minutes in the water I felt comfortable and well-adjusted. I was seeing things that I could not believe were real. The coral reef was beautiful, and the tropical fish were unbelievably colorful and unlike anything I'd ever seen in fresh water. This was the best scuba diving adventure I could have imagined.

Maverick made a few hand signals to indicate that we were past the halfway point on our time window. I knew that we would probably make two stops while resurfacing to avoid decompression sickness. A few moments later I started to feel lightheaded and was getting leg cramps. I sensed that possibly I was suffering from a diving sickness called nitrogen narcosis. Just as I was coming through a small portion of the coral reef, part of my scuba diving equipment got hooked and I was unable to swim any farther. I blacked out.

The next thing I could remember, I was back on the dive boat and Maverick and the divemaster were performing first aid on me. They explained to me that I had become entangled on the reef and had run out of air. I knew by Maverick's ashen, frightened expression that I had been underwater and not breathing for an unknown length of time. The divemaster told me, "Your buddy here went back in with very little air left to rescue you. If he hadn't, you would be dead."

Once I was breathing normally and feeling a little less shaky, I turned to Maverick, who still looked shaken and was stealing glances at me frequently to make sure I was really okay. I grabbed him by the shoulder and looked into his eyes and said, "Mav, you saved my life today. You literally saved my life. Thank you."

When we got back to the resort I decided that I wanted to spend the rest of the vacation on shore. Maverick was disappointed but supportive. On the flight out, Maverick didn't really want to talk. All he said was, "No more Nitrox for you." I agreed wholeheartedly. No more Nitrox for me.

Chapter 43

As I walked into the squad room at the police station, Maverick kept saying one of his famous Maverickisms, "Beautiful day, great to be alive". When he saw me, he reached down, picked up a paper and vigorously waved it in the air, glaring at me.

"Heard you were at the range yesterday. I taught you the right way to shoot but looks to me like you're shooting like Barney Fife. What the fuck happened?" I walked up to him and said, "Didn't you have a bad day at the range last fall?" His eyes narrowed as he glared at me and he said, "Yes, but you'd better get down to the range and practice. Your scores went down by 20% and that is unacceptable." I told him I would get down there and practice.

Maverick quickly shifted out of confrontational mode into chill mode. He said, "We have a case to work; let's give the people of our fine community some justice." I said, "Seems to me sometimes that you only have two gears – belligerence or benevolence. I sure appreciate the second gear. Tell me about the case."

Maverick said, "The chief sent me a memo that there's been some breaking and entering here in the village and in the adjoining community of Prairie Township. Looks like we have some bandits with a real weakness for televisions, guns, drugs and jewelry. The timeline is stretched out for almost two months. We had a few leads on this and I've confirmed with the lieutenant and the chief that this is a high-priority case. I need to go down to Prairie Township and study the evidence."

I said, "That sounds like a good plan. Let's finish up the case we're working here, then have some lunch over in Prairie Township and start the new case." After finishing the case, we drove over to the local diner in Prairie Township, where we met up with an officer from the Prairie Township Police department.

Sergeant Ryan J. Erikson. Ryan was best described as brassy, with a mammoth personality. At times when he spoke, he was so over-the-top that you wondered if maybe he thought he was starring in a movie. The guy was a legend in his own mind.

.

Ryan said, "Have you looked at the weather today? It appears we have a large thunderstorm brewing just west of town. Just our luck it'll end up being a tornado or something."

Maverick and I received a call; we had to run red lights and siren back to the village to answer a trouble with subject call. After completing the call, I walked into the briefing room and looked at the TV. The weather channel was showing a large storm and advised everyone in the path of the storm to take cover due to a possible tornado.

I ran back into the office to tell Maverick about the weather, but he laughed and said, "Probably just a thunderstorm. You're overreacting." About five minutes later, the county sheriff's department came on dispatch, saying, "All units be advised, we have a report of a tornado in the county near Prairie Township. Please follow standard protocol provided by Emergency Management."

Maverick looked at me, saying, "Hey Patty, looks like we're on storm-chasing duty. We need to head out to Prairie Township." Maverick had a gleam in his eye that I rarely see. He relished the opportunity to answer this emergency with courage and determination. I had a sick feeling in my stomach and sensed that we were embarking on a terrible adventure. Maverick jumped into his cruiser, saying, "I'll meet you over at Prairie Township. Let's meet up at the police station there."

As Maverick peeled out of the parking lot of the police station with the lights and siren blaring, I could see that he was on a mission to get over to Prairie Township as soon as possible and warn the people about the tornado. I followed him in my cruiser with a high degree of trepidation.

We were heading over to Prairie Township when County Fire came on the radio stating that the fire department would be staging at the west side of the township. They'd already seen multiple tornadoes, heavy wind and hail. I knew we were in for a big storm. I hit Maverick up on the radio, and he confirmed that he'd heard the report and said that we needed to get there as soon as possible.

As we made our way out of town I was stepping on the accelerator in my cruiser, but all I could see were red and blue lights as Maverick pulled away. I was doing 90 and he must've been doing 120. I couldn't keep up with him. It was so windy it was raining sideways. I decided that I would take the secondary route into Prairie Township because there was a report of trees down on W Avenue.

I heard Larry come on the radio. He said, "All units be advised that the tornado is turning south. All responding units shelter in place."

I tried Maverick on the radio again, asking, "Are you heading down W Avenue?" There was no response. I tried him again, but still no response. A few minutes later I heard Larry back on the radio, "Be advised one of the responding units was caught up in the twister."

A few moments later I heard county dispatch declare 'Radio Silence'. "Calling missing unit in tornado." There was no response. I thought it must be a county sheriff unit that was missing but they kept calling Unit 202. That was the car Maverick was driving. I thought, "I need to get over there and tell them that they have the unit numbers mixed up."

Minutes later, Larry came on the radio and said, "Unit 203, go to tactical channel five." I confirmed and switched channels. Larry asked, "Were you following Maverick over here?" I responded that I had been. He said, "Be advised his cruiser got caught up in the tornado and he is missing in action." Larry said, "I was parked near the top of Pine Bluff as the storm approached. I saw Maverick's cruiser drive down W Avenue, then into the wall of debris." I swallowed hard and said, "Let's meet somewhere and form a search party." Larry said that he would meet me at Fire Station 15 in Prairie Township, where the emergency manager was setting up a temporary command center. I said, "Be there in ten." When I arrived at the fire station I saw more long faces than ever before, and many people busy preparing equipment and receiving duty assignments.

The emergency manager had arrived on site and was setting up a command post at the fire station. He said, "To my best understanding, the tornado came into town from the west and cut a path about 300 yards wide by two miles long. Probably affected over 700 structures."

Gerald B. Strouse. Emergency Manager of the county. Gerald was known for his dedication to emergency management. He was an unfortunate-looking man, with a strange lump over his Adam's apple when he spoke. On occasion he waddled a bit like a duck due to some type of foot disorder. He was known for his lifeless face, lack of animation and cast-iron backbone. He had an unnatural expression on his face that made him appear to be a tortured soul.

I asked Gerald, "What about Unit 202, Maverick?" Gerald said, "Low survival potential. We have many people trapped under debris; they come first. After we have searched the houses in the tornado's path we will search other areas." I was angry but accepted my duty assignment and followed directions. The grid search assignment was the 500 block of Best Street to the water tower. I knew there were 30-plus houses in my duty assignment. I thought, "I will complete the assignment, then circle back to the place where Larry last saw Maverick's cruiser."

As I searched my area I found more survivors than expected. This renewed my hope that Maverick survived, but then my hope sank every time I found a deceased victim. As I got to the end of Best Street I noticed that the water tower had been damaged by the tornado and one of the support beams was broken and rattling when the wind blew. I called it in to the radio at Emergency Management, but no one really cared. They were preoccupied with medical triage.

I finished my assignment and floored it to the 16000 block of W Avenue. I parked the cruiser and ran out into the field where Maverick's cruiser was last seen. I fell to my knees, looked up at the sky and cried out, "God, please help me!"

Larry pulled up on the street behind me and, though he obviously saw my display of emotion, I was too upset to give a damn. We spoke for a moment. He said, "300 yards from here I saw him drive into the debris wall of the tornado, and he was gone." Larry's hands shook, and his eyes watered as he spoke, not wanting me to see him cry. In a choked voice he said, "I'm heading back up to town to get a new assignment." Larry jumped into his cruiser and floored the accelerator.

Just then my cell phone rang. I was pretty sure that the cell service was out, and the cell tower had been knocked down, but somehow the cell signal got through. I looked down at the caller ID and saw that it was the chief. He was angry, bellowing into the phone, "We have a natural disaster in the area and you and Maverick drove directly into the path of the tornado; what the fuck ever possessed you to do something so foolish?"

I finally interrupted the chief and said, "I apologize for what happened, but we need to put our heads together and find Maverick. The last time I talked to Emergency Management, they had Maverick declared missing in action and presumed dead." The chief caught his breath and I could hear him making some noises on the other end of the phone. I wasn't certain, but I thought he might be trying not to cry. The chief said, "I called you on the radio, but you weren't answering." I'm sorry, Chief," I said. "My radio was on tactical channel five and not on the prime channel. I apologize for forgetting to change back to the prime channel. I'm resetting my radio and heading back to get a new duty assignment right now."

The chief told me, "The state police helicopter is up in the air and coming soon. After they do their first review of the damage there will be a new list of priorities. You better get down to the Emergency Management center and get in line for a new duty assignment." He went on to say that he and the lieutenant were suiting up and on their way to Prairie Township.

As I got back into my cruiser to head up to town I heard Larry on the radio reporting that he had found a new debris field just east of the cemetery that appeared to be pieces of houses and cars, and possibly a police vehicle. I was compelled by direct orders of the chief to head back up to the Emergency Management station but, at the same time, I couldn't keep myself from driving by this new debris field. If I could find any piece of Maverick's cruiser I would emotionally accept that Maverick was lost, and I would continue with the search for survivors.

When I arrived at the debris field I saw large piles of tree branches and brush. This looked like the place the tornado started dumping what it picked up near town. The whole field looked like a war zone – complete chaos. As I walked to the debris field I thought the tornado must've torn up at least half of the town and that it would probably be a month or two before things would get back to normal. I searched through the field, finding a lot of lawn furniture and household stuff. I searched up and down the field many times, determined to find Maverick, dead or alive.

As I turned the corner around one of the debris piles I saw the chief and Lieutenant Dan. The chief was clearly angry, and I braced myself, waiting for him to start yelling at me. Instead, his voice was very low and shaking with suppressed anger. He said, "You defied my direct orders. I told you to go to Emergency Management. We have limited resources here and I don't want you at the scene. It's only going to complicate the matter." I did my best to gather my composure. I shook my head and said, "What about Maverick?" The chief said, "Maverick being missing is my problem. Not your problem. Go directly back to Emergency Management right now and get in line for a new assignment. That's a direct order." I was fucking furious.

I said to the chief, "Sir, I have total respect for you and for your position but considering the situation I would rather have you fire me than go back up to Emergency Management." The chief looked at the ground, then at Lieutenant Dan. The lieutenant took me aside and said, "I believe that you're overwhelmed and that your stress level is causing you to make decisions that are not rational. It's my responsibility to relieve you of your duties. This is a direct order; you're officially off duty. Drive back to the police station, go off duty and go home. I will call you in for a post-incident review of your conduct. You're officially off duty until further notice."

I knew what that meant – suspended without pay. I said to Lieutenant Dan, in a discouraged voice, "Yes sir, I will follow your orders." I got back into my cruiser and started heading back to the village. When I got back, I shut off my radio. I was walking through the squad room when it occurred to me that I should write the chief and the lieutenant an email stating the reasons behind my decisions. I thought I should take total accountability for my actions and the results.

I sent the email and was about to walk out the door when the phone rang. I was unable to stop myself from picking up the phone. I took a deep breath and said, "Can I help you?" Larry, in a panicked voice, asked, "What in the hell are you doing over there?" I told him that the chief and the lieutenant had sent me off duty.

"Are you aware of what's happened over here? First there was the tornado, and then the wind knocked the water tower over. Approximately 800,000 gallons of water came gushing out and ran down Best Street into the ravine just west of the cemetery. Two members of the Prairie Township fire department who were on the highway overpass saw a large wall of water wash by, and that wall of water knocked the chief and the lieutenant into the Sawyer River. The firefighters were unable to get to them before they were washed away."

I told Larry that I wasn't willing to challenge the chief's orders. I heard Larry shout something at the sheriff and the sheriff shouted back. Larry spoke forcefully into the phone, "The sheriff is overriding the chief's orders. Suit up, get your gear on and get your ass over here soon as possible."

As I walked downstairs into the locker room to get my uniform on, I stared into the large full-length mirror. When I looked into my own eyes they were empty. I took a quick inventory of my thoughts. Investigation, storm, tornado, Maverick missing, altercation with the chief, taken off duty, phone call with Larry, back on duty, and now the chief and the lieutenant missing. What a fucking day.

Chapter 44

A calm washed over me. I felt duty call and I experienced a quick resurgence of energy and focus. As I pulled up to Fire Station 15, I saw that they had made some progress while I was gone. The situation still seemed fluid and there was still a high level of chaos.

I walked right past Gerald, the emergency manager, and went up to Larry, saying, "I need you to give me a quick briefing on our current situation." Larry said, "I have two pieces of information. First, the chief and the lieutenant. A helicopter is above Sawyer River looking for them. The second part I don't think you want to hear. Members of the fire department have found a rear deck lid from a police vehicle. The unit number on the deck lid is 202. I saw it myself. I believe it's all that's left of Maverick's cruiser.

My head started to pound, and my stomach felt like it dropped right down to my knees. I shook my head in disbelief, saying repeatedly, "I don't believe you. I need to see the deck lid myself." We walked out into the field behind the fire station. I saw a lot of brush and debris. After about a two-minute walk, Larry showed me the deck lid of a police vehicle. I looked at it closely and said to him, "Yep, that's it. Maverick is gone."

Suddenly ten years of experiences and memories of working with Maverick flashed through my mind like a slow-motion movie or a succession of snapshots and feelings. It was a hell of a trip down memory lane. I felt like I had aged several years in a matter of moments. When I snapped out of my daydream, Larry looked angry and was saying, "It's time for you to pull yourself together and get back to work."

As I walked back up to the front of the fire station to get a new assignment, I saw an Amish horse and buggy pull up. A young Amish man was driving the buggy. He hopped out and was waving his hat in the air, exclaiming, "You will never believe what I found in my back yard after the storm cleared!"

Still in shock from seeing the proof that Maverick was gone, I greeted him. He walked me around to the back of the buggy and opened the back-curtain window. There was a young Amish girl, maybe 12 years old, holding a man's head and shoulders in her lap. Tears were pouring down her face and she kept whispering the same prayer repeatedly – "Yea, though I walk through the valley of the shadow of death, I will fear no evil: for Thou art with me." She took the hem of her skirt and wiped the dirt off the man's face and when I got a direct look at him I couldn't believe my eyes. It was Maverick, and he was alive!

Maverick was alive but badly injured. He looked as though he was near death and appeared to have been dragged feet first through a dark loamy swamp. His uniform was shredded and there was dirt, mud and dust all over his body. One of his eyes was swollen shut and there was so much dirt and dust packed into his nostrils that he made a strange noise when he tried to breathe.

Looking at Maverick, an indescribable joy washed through my soul and I was willing to do anything to get Maverick to the hospital alive. I ran around the corner of the firehouse and shouted at the paramedics, "Bring me a stretcher; we have a priority one medical condition we need to stabilize for transport." Moments later I was helping to get Maverick out of the buggy and onto the stretcher.

Doing my initial patient survey of Maverick, I realized that he had a severe concussion, multiple lacerations, a bilateral femur fracture and multiple potentially fatal injuries. Gerald from Emergency Management walked up. I pointed at Maverick and I looked Gerald in the eye and said, "You were wrong." His usually stony face crumpled as he looked down at his feet and waddled away like a duck. As he was walking away I frantically shouted, "Gerald! Call the helicopter on the radio and get them here to transport Maverick." He reluctantly turned around, stared at me with his stony face, and then after a short pause he said softly, "Yes, sir."

Chapter 45

As the firefighters set up the landing zone I could hear the helicopter approaching. I had Maverick stabilized on the backboard and gurney. I got him to mumble a few barely audible words that made no sense as he was in and out of consciousness. All I could think of was to speak a few 'Maverickisms' in his ear, like "beautiful day, great to be alive" or "show up wearing a bell and tell 'em to go to hell". Finally, I said, "Watch out, stand by, get out of my way, and be advised – I'm in charge." His eyes fluttered a few times and the corners of his mouth turned up. I knew he couldn't talk, but he could hear me. I kept telling him in a stern voice, "Hang in there. The helicopter is coming. We're going to get you to the hospital." As the state police helicopter hovered down from above tree level it kicked up a large amount of dirt, dust and small brush.

I had a brief conversation on the ground with the pilot and co-pilot. I asked them if they had spotted anybody in the river, like the chief or lieutenant. They said they hadn't had time to complete a search. I explained to them that we needed to get Maverick to the nearest hospital. The pilot said, "This is really a search and rescue helicopter. It's not set up for medical transport. If this doesn't work it's on you, not me." I said, "I take accountability for all liabilities."

As we were getting ready to take off, I shouted at the pilot to wait a minute. I had seen Glen Rawlings from the fire department pull up in Engine 1611. I jumped out and waved him over. I said, "I need you to help me transport Maverick to the hospital via the helicopter."

He shook his head and said, "No, I'm not authorized to do that.' I said, "I know you'll get in trouble with the fire chief and Emergency Management, but I will answer for that." He thought for a moment, then reluctantly agreed and jumped into the helicopter with his equipment. After takeoff, Glen started patient care, getting an IV started and assessing vital signs. After a few rounds of vitals, Glen said that Maverick's vital signs were weakening, and the situation was acute.

I was stuck by the window as we crossed the Sawyer River, my eyes glued to the terrain. The Sawyer River was a fast-moving whitewater river with many rocks near the surface. At a certain point near town, the river was 50 yards across and not possible to swim most times of the year. I said to the pilot, "Circle around; I see something in the river." The helicopter banked and lowered down to the river.

As we got closer, I saw someone clinging to a large cluster of logs and debris caught on the rocks, but I couldn't make out who it was. As we got closer I recognized the chief. I glanced back at Glen and said, "I'm going to have to throw you in the river to get the chief." He yelled, "No fucking way am I going down there!" I said, "Hey, you know swift water rescue better than I do. You've thrown enough people in the river. I've seen you do it." Glen looked puzzled. I said, "Remember that time we were training water rescue? You threw Carl in the river, then lassoed him and pulled him to the shore." I added, "He never really forgave you for that one. Make up for it by going in and getting the chief. C'mon, Glen. I need you. Do it."

Glen looked around in the helicopter, found a rescue harness and said, "What the fuck." As I was preparing Glen to go out on the wire, I heard the pilot on the radio to Emergency Management. They dispatched a fire truck by ground to assist us. I threw some rope at Glen and said tie this rope around the Chief and tie it into your carabiners. When you clap your hands above your head I will reel you two in. As Glen was about to exit the door of the helicopter, I shouted into his ear, "You truly are the most courageous firefighter I know." Glen shook his head and shouted back, "Yeah, I know. And when this fucking mess is over you really owe me one."

As I was lowering Glen down on the wire, the co-pilot came back and said, "What in the hell is going on? I thought we were going to finish the medical transport before we went back to search and rescue. "Your decisions are really pissing the pilot off." Ignoring him, I lowered Glen down onto the cluster of logs. The counter-torque from the helicopter blades began spinning Glen on the wire. I was pretty sure that at a few points I saw vomit flying out of his mouth. As he got close, he hit the water in the river behind the logs. The pilot repositioned the helicopter, finally landing him on the logs. It looked like a rough ride.

When Glen got to the chief, the chief was moving his mouth and his hands furiously, clearly upset. Glen looked angry and ignored the chief, then tied the rope around his torso and to the carabiner on his rescue harness. I couldn't make out much more with the helicopter bouncing around fiercely in the wind.

Glen got his hands above his head and started clapping. I hit the control button on the winch to raise them up to the helicopter. The winch started to come up and then made a strange grinding noise. I yelled to the co-pilot, who came back, checked out the winch and stated that the winch was broken. I said, "What do we do now?" As the co-pilot started to work on the winch, I looked over my shoulder and saw that Maverick was gasping for breath and had started to have convulsions.

When I looked at Maverick on the backboard I could see that one of his pupils was constricted; this was a sign that he had brain swelling, or cerebral edema. From previous experience, I knew that he was just minutes from death. I took a moment to do some triage. When I did the math in my head, I didn't like the answer I came up with. Maverick was probably going to die, and my best chance for any success was to get the chief and Glen out of the water.

The co-pilot and I struggled with the controls for the winch. We worked on the wire, lowered it down, but every time we tried to raise it, the winch made that same grinding noise. I asked the co-pilot, "What are the chances that we can get Glen and the chief back up into the helicopter?" He paused for a moment, looked out the window and said, "Maybe ten percent."

I asked the co-pilot, "What the fuck should we do now? We're stuck over the river with a broken winch, and my buddy Maverick is dying. What do you suggest we do now?" The co-pilot said, "We're going to have to do an emergency cutaway procedure. I've trained for this, but I don't know how things are going to go for the people on the ground. One of two things could happen – one, the wire could come down from the helicopter and strike them, injuring or killing them; or two, possibly the wind will blow the cable to the side and they can cut away from the carabiner on the ground and the wire will go into the river. The co-pilot opened one of the cabinet doors in the helicopter and brought out the cable cutter.

I glanced back out the door at Glen and the chief. It didn't look very good. My heart was pounding, and I was afraid the cable was going to come down and kill them. As I looked out the window of the helicopter to the east, I could see a firetruck and ambulance approaching down a dirt road west of Broad Ripple Boulevard. I could see that they were less than a mile away, and I felt reassured that, if we did the cutaway, the firefighters on the ground could get a rope out to the chief and Glen and get them to shore.

Chapter 46

I said a quick prayer as the co-pilot cut the cable, and I suddenly realized that if the chief did survive, I probably would be fired. Seconds after we cut the cable, the co-pilot went back to the cockpit. The pilot slammed the throttle and twisted the cycler, and we floored it off to the hospital.

As I shut the door of the helicopter, my attention shifted back to Maverick. He'd started to come out of convulsions. He was breathing, but his pulse and blood pressure were weak. I was terrified he was going to die. I screamed at the pilot, "Get this damn helicopter to the hospital!"

Within ten minutes I could make out Lakeside Community Hospital. The ER had ambulances stacked on the service road leading to the entrance of the ER, but the helipad was empty, and we were making our approach to land. After landing we carried Maverick on the gurney into the hospital. The ER was a madhouse because of the tornado.

The pilot tapped me on the shoulder. When I turned around, he pointed at me and said, "Hey, buddy, this is a one-way ride for you and your friend. We're done here. I hope he makes it." As if they had choreographed it, the pilot and co-pilot turned sharply 180 degrees and walked away briskly toward the helicopter.

I approached the charge nurse and pleaded with her to make Maverick a priority one triage patient. She checked Maverick out and said, "Yes. Wheel him down to room seven." A few moments later a doctor and two nurses walked in. I gave them a summary that Maverick had been caught up in the tornado and had a concussion, bilateral femur fracture, his pulse and blood pressure were weak, he'd been convulsing in the helicopter, and his pupils were unequal, suggesting bleeding on the brain. The doctor shook his head and said, "So that sounds like a bizarre story. Let's get to work on him and see if we can save his life." I gave Maverick's emergency contact information – his wife, Helen – to the nurse and asked her to have someone call Helen and tell her to get here right away.

A nurse took me aside and said, "There is a police officer in the next room who is wearing the same uniform as yours. We have him sedated. A couple of teenage boys said they scooped him up out of the river. Can you help us figure out who he is?" "Of course," I replied. When I walked in the room I couldn't believe it. Lying in the bed was my Lieutenant Dan. He looked like he had been to hell and back; his uniform was muddy and shredded, and he looked like he had ridden some of the debris down the river. The nurse had him hooked up to a heart monitor and pulse oximeter. It was obvious he was critically injured.

I told the nurse, "This is Lieutenant Isaac Daniel Davison, better known as Lieutenant Dan. He works with me at the police department. His wife's name is Isabella. Call the Village Police Department and the secretary will give you her number." The nurse was shuffling multiple charts simultaneously and trying to type all the information into the laptop computer. It took her 20 minutes to get all the information.

I heard a familiar voice in the hallway. I didn't want to go out there, but my curiosity won out. As I walked out of Lieutenant Dan's room, the chief was on a gurney just down the hall. I had mixed feelings but forced myself to face the music. As I walked up to his gurney he looked at me with shock and disgust. The chief looked disheveled and emotionally bankrupt. His first question was, "Were you in the helicopter?" I told him that I had been in the helicopter and tried to rescue him. "Why did you leave us?" he asked. I said that the winch had broken after I lowered Glen down to the river. He was very annoyed but swallowed his emotion. He said, "This is neither the time nor place to discuss this matter. When this emergency is over we're going to have a long talk in my office." I said that I understood.

I started to say that Maverick and Lieutenant Dan were there in the ER too when I heard running footsteps and someone screaming my name in the hall. I turned around to see Glen, livid and looking for revenge, less than 50 feet away. Glen was bellowing, "Joe, you bastard! You left me in the river to drown!" I put my hands up and started to explain that the winch broke, but he wasn't looking for a conversation. When he got close enough he threw a right jab, striking me straight in the chin. I fell straight backward, landing on my head. I saw some sparks and then I was out.

Chapter 47

I woke up in a hospital bed to find the chief standing near my bed. I asked, "Did you recover quickly, or have I been out a long time?" "No, just 20 minutes or so," replied the chief. He said the doctor had checked him out and declared him a little banged up, but okay for discharge. The chief said that Glen Rawlings was on his way back to the Emergency Management station for now, but he asked whether I wanted to press assault and battery charges against Glen for socking me in the jaw and giving me a concussion. "No, Chief, I really don't want to do that. Glen's not a bad guy; he just has a short temper. And considering the fact that he went into the river to rescue you, you might want to cut him some slack. I wanted to rescue you, but I didn't have the strength and courage to do it. Glen stepped up, put on the harness, and went down there on the wire to save your life."

"It's up to you to decide how to handle it," I continued, "but if it were up to me, I would rather handle it internally by having the fire chief write Glen up and put him on probation for a year, or however long the fire chief sees fit. And I'm sure that, after Glen has time to cool down and reflect, he'll apologize to me. I'll accept his apology and we'll move on; it won't get in the way of our working together or keep me from trusting him in the future."

"I disagree with the way you want to handle it," said the chief. "I think you're too accepting of Glen's misconduct, but if you want it handled internally, I'll talk to the fire chief about it as soon as I get out of here. I don't think I'd be so forgiving, but you're the guy who got punched in the face, so I'll go along with it. I'll ask the fire chief to make it clear to Glen that it was your decision to not press charges."

The chief looked at me for a few moments with a troubled expression on his face, so I knew there was more that he wanted to say. I said, "Chief, there's more, isn't there? What is it?" The chief took a deep breath and said, "Joe, there's no easy way to say this. Lieutenant Dan didn't make it." My eyes began to tear up, and I asked in a choked voice, "What happened? He looked like he was going to be okay when I saw him." The chief replied, "He went into shock. The water in his lungs and the pressure on his heart caused him to go into cardiac arrest. The doctors did everything they could, but they couldn't save him. Thankfully, your identifying Dan when you did made it possible for Isabella to get here and spend some time with him before he died. The doctors have told her that he didn't make it, but I need to talk with her and let her know just how much Dan meant to all of us as a department and as individuals."

The chief turned to leave, then turned back and added, "Oh, and Maverick is in surgery for probably another 30 minutes or so. He's stable and expected to survive. And Joe, I realize that Maverick would be dead now if you hadn't taken the actions that you took. I understand why you had to cut the cable in the helicopter, and I'm very glad that you got Maverick here in time; however, we do still need to conduct a post-incident review." I replied, "I understand."

"I'm heading back to the station to put on a clean uniform and go pay my respects to Isabella. If you are released from the hospital today, make sure you're in my office first thing in the morning for that review," said the chief, not unkindly. I nodded my understanding.

Chapter 48

I was crushed that Lieutenant Dan hadn't survived, yet at the same time I was excited and happy that Maverick was going to pull through. I'd been afraid that his injuries were too extensive and that I'd never get to see him alive again. The ER doctor came in just then and said that, other than a mild concussion and a bruised jaw where Glen hit me, I was just fine and could be discharged, but I was to take the rest of the day off because of the concussion. Once I signed the discharge paperwork and left the ER, I went looking for the surgery waiting room. When I found it, Helen was there talking with the surgeon. I held back to give them some privacy, but Helen motioned me over, telling the surgeon that I was the reason her husband was alive.

As the surgeon left, Helen hugged me, saying, "Thank you, Patty. You saved my husband's life, and I will always be grateful to you." She told me that her husband had a long road ahead of him, but that ultimately, he was expected to make a full recovery. She said the surgeon had told her to expect Maverick to be off work for up to three months or so while he recuperated, and we both laughed about how badly he would take being away from the station for that long. I asked Helen if I could wait with her for Maverick to be moved to a room, and she said, "Of course! I know Steve will want to see you after all you two have been through." Just then, the nurse came in and told Helen she could go see Maverick in the recovery room, so I got a cup of stale coffee from the coffeemaker in the surgery waiting room and sat down to wait for her.

A while later, after Maverick had been moved to a private room, Helen and I went down to see him. He had a whole host of injuries, some internal and some external, and had so many bandages on that I might not have recognized him had he not smiled faintly and said, "Beautiful day; great day to be alive." Even after just coming out of surgery, he was still spouting his Maverickisms.

Maverick said to me, "Patty, come closer. I need to tell you something." I moved over next to his bed, and he grabbed my hand and said the exact words I'd said to him in Mexico, "You saved my life today. You literally saved my life. Thank you." I couldn't help it; my tears started to fall. Maverick went on, "Those are the exact words you said to me after your scuba diving accident, and today you returned the favor. I will never forget what you've done for me." Helen moved closer and took my other hand, saying, "And I will never forget what you've done for me and the kids. Thank you so much, Patty." I said, "There was no way that I wasn't going to do everything in my power to save my best friend."

At Maverick's request, I filled him in on what had happened – the tornado, the water tower collapsing, the Amish buggy rescue, the state police helicopter, the attempt to save the chief on the way to the hospital, and finally, Lieutenant Dan's death. Maverick was understandably very emotional to hear that the lieutenant hadn't survived, and I decided he'd heard more than enough for now. "Helen, Maverick…you two need some time alone and I need to get home and get some rest. I'm meeting with the chief first thing in the morning and I want to be on top of my game. I'm going to take off now, but I'll be seeing you very soon." They both thanked me again, and I left to see if there were any ambulance drivers left in the ER who could give me a lift back to the Emergency Management station to get my truck.

Chapter 49

After hitching a ride back to the Emergency Management station with one of the ambulance drivers, I got in my truck, picked up some fast-food dinner through a drive-through, and went home exhausted and drained. I sat in front of the tv eating my dinner and watching the news, but everything was about the tornado, the last thing in the world I wanted to think about right then. I decided to go to bed and get a good night's sleep before facing the chief the next day.

When I walked into the station the next morning, the grief over the loss of Lieutenant Dan was palpable. He had been an integral part of our police force, a colleague and trusted friend. The flag out front was at half-staff, and everyone was given a black ribbon banner to attach to their badges to honor Lieutenant Dan. The sadness was as thick as molasses.

I saw that the chief was in his office, and I knocked, asking if this was a good time to talk. He smiled and said, "C'mon in. We might as well get this damn thing over with. Close the door." I sat down across from the chief and waited to hear what he had to say. "Joe, I think you're a good cop and a good human being. I believe that everyone has the right to make one mistake a year and have it forgiven by God. As long as that person has the wisdom to share that mistake with God, the calendar year starts over. Still, having said that, I have to write you up for dereliction of duty and refusal to obey direct orders. It will stay in your file for 90 days and if there are no more incidents, I will remove it, destroy it, and we will forget that it ever happened." I smiled in relief and thanked him.

Switching gears, the chief said, "After a near-death experience in the river, and given that I'm in my late sixties, I've decided the time has come for me to retire and turn this department over to a new generation of police officers. According to Maverick's doctors, he should be able to return to work within the next 90 days, and I will need to determine if he's able to take over as the new chief. I won't be retiring until I know that I have a new chief ready to step in. That also leaves open a position for a new lieutenant; I don't know if you're ready for it, but let me know if you have anyone you'd like to refer for the position." "Yes," I replied without hesitation. "Gabriella Bridges. Gabby. She's a lieutenant at the sheriff's department and went through the academy with me. Do you remember her?" "I do remember her," said the chief. "Have her come in and submit an application if she's interested."

"On to more pressing – and depressing – matters," said the chief. "We have to plan a funeral with full honors for Lieutenant Dan. I've been contacted by the Marine Corps, and they would like to be involved in whatever we plan. I'd like you to head up the project. Pull whoever you think you need when you need them; I'll let everyone know in the morning briefing that they can expect that, at some point in the planning, you may need their assistance and that I expect them to cooperate with you. I want to honor Dan the way he deserved to be honored, and you'll need to keep his wife, Isabella, in the loop." He reached in his desk drawer and pulled out a business card. Handing it to me, he said, "This is your contact at the Marine Corps. He's expecting to hear from you today to get the ball rolling. Just remember – full honors."

Chapter 50

After a week of intense planning, the day of Lieutenant Dan's funeral had arrived. I was especially on edge because I'd been given the tremendous responsibility of planning a funeral for a fallen officer and I knew that expectations were high, within both the police department and the Marines. The pallbearers would be Marines on one side and police officers on the other; there would be two honor guards, one police and one military, and we were expecting representatives of police, sheriff and fire departments from all over Michigan and Northern Indiana. Dan's casket would be draped with a flag that would be folded by the pallbearers, handed to the chief, and then presented to Isabella, Dan's wife. Rehearsals had been taking place all week to make sure that everyone knew their place and their part, and everything would go off without a hitch.

The day of the funeral, I was surprised to see Maverick arrive, in uniform, in one of the fire department's first response vehicles. He was in a wheelchair. I hadn't had a chance to talk to Maverick all week with everything that was going on, and I was beyond happy to see him. He was swarmed by fellow officers wishing him well, and I waited until the crowd had dispersed to talk to him. I wheeled him into an interrogation room for a quick chat. "Mav, I'm so happy to see you. You've got to be in a lot of pain, though," I said. He replied, "Yes, this isn't the most comfortable position for me, but I couldn't miss Lieutenant Dan's funeral." "Have you talked to the chief since you got out of the hospital?" I asked. "No," Maverick replied. "I assumed he was crazy busy like you've been." I said that the chief had been very busy and then, lowering my voice, I told Maverick, "Just between you and me, the chief has decided to retire. He's looking at you as his possible replacement. I recommended Gabby as a possible lieutenant."

Maverick's face lit up with a big smile, and he thanked me for the heads up. I told him to keep it to himself and just let the chief come to him to broach the subject when he was ready. "Ok, it's about time to get this funeral going. There will be a procession from the station to the church, then from the church to the cemetery. Full honors, the whole works. We've been rehearsing it all week. By the way, I'll get you a black ribbon banner for your badge."

I was awe-struck by the sight of all the police, sheriff and fire vehicles lined up outside the station and down the street as far as I could see. The procession was led by the hearse carrying Lieutenant Dan's flag-draped coffin, followed by a limousine containing Dan's wife, son and parents; after that was the chief, the rest of the department, representatives of the Marine Corps, the sheriff's department, the fire department, and then representatives of departments from all over the state.

The funeral service was very formal, with a touching eulogy by the chief and a 21-bells ceremony.

After the procession to the cemetery, the pallbearers ceremoniously removed the flag from Lieutenant Dan's casket, folded it precisely into a perfect triangle, then handed it off to the chief. The chief, holding the folded flag with one hand underneath it and the other hand on top, turned smartly and walked up to Dan's widow, Isabella. He quietly said some words of condolence to Isabella, then handed her the flag, turned again and returned to his seat. At that point there was a 3-volley gun salute to conclude the graveside ceremony. Everyone returned to their vehicles and moved on to the luncheon reception.

At the reception, I noticed the chief talking very seriously with Maverick. I saw Maverick nodding as the chief spoke, and then the two shook hands. Once the chief had walked away, I carried two plates of food over to Maverick so we could eat and talk. I set the plates down on the table and asked, "Well?" Maverick said, "It just happened." "What happened?" I asked. Maverick paused for what seemed an eternity, then said, "He just offered me his job. I'm gonna be the chief once I'm back to work full-time. I will expect you to start calling me 'Sir' immediately." "Congratulations, Mav!" I exclaimed. "That's the best news I've heard in a long time!" Replied Maverick, "Well, I still have to be off work for a while, so it will give me plenty of time to think of things I'd like to change. Maybe you can come over and we'll put our heads together like we used to and come up with a wish list." "You got it, Mav," I said. "Say the word and I'll be there."

Maverick broke into a broad grin and said, "The name is 'Sir' – and don't you forget it."

Made in the USA
Monee, IL
03 September 2020

40876819R00115